Praise for the #1 **New York Times**
bestselling In Death series

"Sexy, gritty, richly imagined suspense."

—*Publishers Weekly*

"Groundbreaking." —*The Romance Reader*

"Another taut, gut-wrenching, compelling thriller from the incomparable J. D. Robb (Nora Roberts). Each new install-ment in this series adds more layers to already complex, fascinating characters. And the storylines are always first-rate. Need I say more—another masterpiece!"

—*ParaNormal Romance Reviews*

"Tough-talking thriller with a matchless pace."

—*Kirkus Reviews*

"A well-written, action-packed book that has surprises in it that keep you enthralled till the last sentence of the last page . . . Watching the characters and their rapport develop has been delightful to behold. Ms. Robb has yet again shown what a great suspense author she is. Well done!"

—*The Romance Readers Connection*

"Fast-paced romantic suspense." —*The Best Reviews*

"A unique blend of hard-core police drama, science fiction and passionate romance." —*Gothic Journal*

"Fantastic." —*The Paperback Forum*

Nora Roberts & J. D. Robb

REMEMBER WHEN

Nora Roberts

HOT ICE	SANCTUARY
SACRED SINS	HOMEPORT
BRAZEN VIRTUE	THE REEF
SWEET REVENGE	RIVER'S END
PUBLIC SECRETS	CAROLINA MOON
GENUINE LIES	THE VILLA
CARNAL INNOCENCE	MIDNIGHT BAYOU
DIVINE EVIL	THREE FATES
HONEST ILLUSIONS	BIRTHRIGHT
PRIVATE SCANDALS	NORTHERN LIGHTS
HIDDEN RICHES	BLUE SMOKE
TRUE BETRAYALS	ANGELS FALL
MONTANA SKY	

Series

Circle Trilogy

MORRIGAN'S CROSS

In the Garden Trilogy

BLUE DAHLIA

BLACK ROSE

RED LILY

Key Trilogy

KEY OF LIGHT

KEY OF KNOWLEDGE

KEY OF VALOR

Three Sisters Island Trilogy

DANCE UPON THE AIR

HEAVEN AND EARTH

FACE THE FIRE

Gallaghers of Ardmore Trilogy

JEWELS OF THE SUN

TEARS OF THE MOON

HEART OF THE SEA

Born In Trilogy

BORN IN FIRE

BORN IN ICE

BORN IN SHAME

Chesapeake Bay Saga

SEA SWEPT

RISING TIDES

INNER HARBOR

CHESAPEAKE BLUE

Dream Trilogy

DARING TO DREAM

HOLDING THE DREAM

FINDING THE DREAM

Interlude in Death

J. D. ROBB

BERKLEY BOOKS, NEW YORK

THE BERKLEY PUBLISHING GROUP
Published by the Penguin Group
Penguin Group (USA) Inc.
375 Hudson Street, New York, New York 10014, USA
Penguin Group (Canada), 90 Eglinton Avenue East, Suite 700, Toronto, Ontario M4P 2Y3, Canada
(a division of Pearson Penguin Canada Inc.)
Penguin Books Ltd., 80 Strand, London WC2R 0RL, England
Penguin Group Ireland, 25 St. Stephen's Green, Dublin 2, Ireland (a division of Penguin Books Ltd.)
Penguin Group (Australia), 250 Camberwell Road, Camberwell, Victoria 3124, Australia
(a division of Pearson Australia Group Pty. Ltd.)
Penguin Books India Pvt. Ltd., 11 Community Centre, Panchsheel Park, New Delhi—110 017, India
Penguin Group (NZ), Cnr. Airborne and Rosedale Roads, Albany, Auckland 1310, New Zealand
(a division of Pearson New Zealand Ltd.)
Penguin Books (South Africa) (Pty.) Ltd., 24 Sturdee Avenue, Rosebank, Johannesburg 2196,
South Africa

Penguin Books Ltd., Registered Offices: 80 Strand, London WC2R 0RL, England

Previously included in the anthology *Out of This World*, published by Jove Books, an imprint of The
Berkley Publishing Group.

This is a work of fiction. Names, characters, places, and incidents either are the product of the author's
imagination or are used fictitiously, and any resemblance to actual persons, living or dead, business
establishments, events, or locales is entirely coincidental.

INTERLUDE IN DEATH

A Berkley Book / published by arrangement with the author

PRINTING HISTORY
Berkley edition / March 2006

Copyright © 2001 by Nora Roberts.

ISBN: 0-425-21062-6

BERKLEY®
Berkley Books are published by The Berkley Publishing Group,
a division of Penguin Group (USA) Inc.,
375 Hudson Street, New York, New York 10014.
BERKLEY is a registered trademark of Penguin Group (USA) Inc.
The "B" design is a trademark belonging to Penguin Group (USA) Inc.

PRINTED IN THE UNITED STATES OF AMERICA

10 9 8 7 6 5 4 3 2 1

Learning is not child's play;
we cannot learn without pain.
—ARISTOTLE

Happy is the child whose father
goes to the devil.
—SIXTEENTH-CENTURY PROVERB

1

The faces of murder were varied and complex. Some were as old as time and the furrows scoring them filled with the blood spilled by Cain. One brother's keeper was another's executioner.

Of course, it had been rather elementary to close that particular case. The list of suspects had been, after all, pretty limited.

But time had populated the earth until by the early spring of 2059 it so crawled with people that they spilled out from their native planet to jam man-made worlds and satellites. The skill and ability to create their own worlds, the sheer nerve to consider doing so, hadn't stopped them from killing their brothers.

The method was sometimes more subtle, often more vicious, but people being people could, just as easily, fall back on ramming a sharpened stick through another's heart over a nice patch of lettuce.

The centuries, and man's nature, had developed more than alternative ways to kill and a variety of victims and motives. They had created the need and the means to punish the guilty.

The punishing of the guilty and the demand for justice for the innocent became—perhaps had been since that first extreme case of sibling rivalry—an art and a science.

These days, murder got you more than a short trip to the Land of Nod. It shut you up in a steel and concrete cage where you'd have plenty of time to think about where you went wrong.

But getting the sinner where justice deemed he belonged was the trick. It required a system. And the system demanded its rules, techniques, manpower, organizations, and loopholes.

And the occasional seminar to educate and inform.

As far as Lieutenant Eve Dallas was concerned, she'd rather face a horde of torked-out chemi-heads than conduct a seminar on murder. At least the chemi-heads wouldn't embarrass you to death.

And as if it wasn't bad enough that she'd been drafted to attend the Interplanetary Law Enforcement and Security Conference, as if it wasn't horrifying enough that her own commander had ordered her to give a seminar, the whole ball of goddamn wax had to take shape off-planet.

Couldn't hold the sucker in New York, Eve thought as she lay facedown on the hotel bed. Just couldn't find one spot on the whole fucking planet that could suit up. Nope, just had to send a bunch of cops and techs out into space.

God, she hated space travel.

And of all the places in the known universe, the site-selection committee had to dump them on the Olympus Resort. Not only was she a cop out of her element, but she was a cop out of her element giving a seminar in one of the conference rooms in one of the ridiculously plush hotels owned by her husband.

It was mortifying.

Sneaky son of a bitch, she thought, and wondered if any of the muscles and bones in her body that had dissolved during landing on Olympus had regenerated. He'd planned it, he'd worked it. And now she was paying for it.

She had to socialize, attend meetings. She had to—dear Christ—give a speech. And in less than a week, she would have to get back on that fancy flying death trap of Roarke's and face the journey home.

Since the idea of that made her stomach turn over, she considered the benefits of living out the rest of her life on Olympus.

How bad could it be?

The place had hotels and casinos and homes, bars, shops. Which meant it had people. When you had people, bless their mercenary hearts, you had crime. You had crime, you needed cops. She could trade in her New York Police and Security badge for an Interplanetary Law Enforcement shield.

"I could work for ILE," she muttered into the bedspread.

"Certainly." On the other side of the room, Roarke finished studying a report on one of his other properties. "After a while, you wouldn't think twice about zipping from planet to space station to satellite. And you'd look charming in one of those blue-and-white uniforms and knee-high boots."

Her little fantasy fizzed. Interplanetary meant, after all, interplanetary. "Kiss my ass."

"All right." He walked over, bent down and laid his lips on her butt. Then began working his way up her back.

Unlike his wife, he was energized by space travel.

"If you think you're getting sex, pal, think again."

"I'm doing a lot of thinking." He indulged himself with the long, lean length of her. When he reached the nape of her neck, he rubbed his lips just below the ends of her short, disordered cap of hair. And feeling her quick shiver, grinned as he flipped her over.

Then he frowned a little, skimming a finger along the shallow dent in her chin. "You're a bit pale yet, aren't you?"

Her deep-golden-brown eyes stared sulkily into his. Her mouth, wide, mobile, twisted into a sneer. "When I'm on my feet again, I'm going to punch you in that pretty face of yours."

"I look forward to it. Meanwhile." He reached down, began unbuttoning her shirt.

"Pervert."

"Thank you, Lieutenant." Because she was his, and it continuously delighted him, he brushed a kiss over her torso, then tugged off her boots, stripped off her trousers. "And I hope we'll get to the perversion part of our program shortly. But for now." He picked her up and carried her out of the bedroom. "I think we'll try a little postflight restorative."

"Why do I have to be naked?"

"I like you naked."

He stepped into a bathroom. No, not a bathroom, Eve

mused. That was too ordinary a word for this oasis of sensual indulgence.

The tub was a lake, deep blue and fed by gleaming silver tubes twined together in flower shapes. Rose trees heavy with saucer-size white blooms flanked the marble stairs that led into a shower area where a waterfall already streamed gently down gleaming walls. The tall cylinders of mood and drying tubes were surrounded by spills of flowers and foliage, and she imagined that anyone using one of them would look like a statue in a garden.

A wall of glass offered a view of cloudless sky turned to gold by the tint of the privacy screen.

He set her down on the soft cushions of a sleep chair and walked to one of the curved counters that flowed around the walls. He slid open a panel in the tiles and set a program on the control pad hidden behind it.

Water began to spill into the tub, the lights dimmed, and music, softly sobbing strings, slid into the air.

"I'm taking a bath?" she asked him.

"Eventually. Relax. Close your eyes."

But she didn't close her eyes. It was too tempting just to watch him as he moved around the room, adding something frothy to the bath, pouring some pale gold liquid into a glass.

He was tall and had an innate sort of grace. Like a cat did, she thought. A big, dangerous cat that only pretended to be tame when it suited his mood. His hair was black and thick and longer than her own. It spilled nearly to his shoulders and provided a perfect frame for a face that made her think of dark angels and doomed poets and ruthless warriors all at once.

When he looked at her with those hot and wildly blue eyes, the love inside her could spread so fast and strong, it hurt her heart to hold it.

He was hers, she thought. Ireland's former bad boy who had made his life, his fortune, his place by hook or—well—by crook.

"Drink this."

He liked to tend her, she mused as she took the glass he offered. She, lost child, hard-ass cop, could never figure out if it irritated or thrilled her. Mostly, she supposed, it just baffled her.

"What is it?"

"Good." He took it back from her, sipped himself to prove it.

When she sampled it, she found that he was right, as usual. He walked behind the chair, the amusement on his face plain when he tipped her back and her gaze narrowed with suspicion. "Close your eyes," he repeated and slipped goggles over her face. "One minute," he added.

Lights bled in front of her closed lids. Deep blues, warm reds in slow, melting patterns. She felt his hands, slicked with something cool and fragrant, knead her shoulders, the knotted muscles of her neck.

Her system, jangled from the flight, began to settle. "Well, this doesn't suck," she murmured, and let herself drift.

He took the glass from her hand as her body slipped into the ten-minute restorative program he'd selected. He'd told her one minute.

He'd lied.

When she was relaxed, he bent to kiss the top of her head, then draped a silk sheet over her. Nerves, he knew, had worn her out. Added to them the stress and fatigue of coming off a difficult case and being shot directly into an off-planet assignment that she detested, and it was no wonder her system was unsettled.

He left her sleeping and went out to see to a few minor details for the evening event. He'd just stepped back in when the timer of the program beeped softly and she stirred.

"Wow." She blinked, scooped at her hair when he set the goggles aside.

"Feel better?"

"Feel great."

"A little travel distress is easy enough to fix. The bath should finish it off."

She glanced over, saw that the tub was full, heaped with bubbles that swayed gently in the current of the jets. "I just bet it will." Smiling, she got up, crossed the room to step down into the sunken pool. And lowering herself neck-deep, she let out a long sigh.

"Can I have that wine or whatever the hell it is?"

"Sure." Obliging, he carried it over, set it on the wide lip behind her head.

"Thanks. I've gotta say, this is some . . ." She trailed off, pressed her fingers to her temple.

"Eve? Headache?" He reached out, concerned, and found himself flipping into the water with her.

When he surfaced, she was grinning, and her hand was cupped possessively between his legs. "Sucker," she said.

"Pervert."

"Oh, yeah. Let me show you how I finish off this little restorative program, ace."

$\mathcal{R}$estored, and smug, she took a quick spin in the drying tube. If she was going to live only a few more days before crashing into a stray meteor and being burned to a cinder by exploding rocket fuel on the flight back home, she might as well make the best of it.

She snagged a robe, wrapped herself in it, and strolled back into the bedroom.

Roarke, already wearing trousers, was scanning what looked like encoded symbols as they scrolled across the screen of the bedroom tele-link. Her dress, at least she assumed it was a dress, was laid out on the bed.

She frowned at the sheer flow of bronze, walked over to finger the material. "Did I pack this?"

"No." He didn't bother to glance back, he could see her suspicious scowl clearly enough in his mind. "You packed several days' worth of shirts and trousers. Summerset made some adjustments in your conference wardrobe."

"Summerset." The name hissed like a snake between her lips. Roarke's major domo was a major pain in her ass. "You let him paw through my clothes? Now I have to burn them."

Though he'd made considerable adjustments to her wardrobe in the past year, there were, in his opinion, several items left that deserved burning. "He rarely paws. We're running a little behind," he added. "The cocktail reception started ten minutes ago."

"Just an excuse for a bunch of cops to get shit-faced. Don't see why I have to get dressed up for it."

"Image, darling Eve. You're a featured speaker and one of the event's VIPs."

"I hate that part. It's bad enough when I have to go to your deals."

"You shouldn't be nervous about your seminar."

"Who said I'm nervous?" She snatched up the dress. "Can you see through this thing?"

His lips quirked. "Not quite."

"*Not quite*" was accurate, she decided. The getup felt thin as a cloud, and that was good for comfort. The flimsy layers of it barely shielded the essentials. Still, as her fashion sense could be etched on a microchip with room to spare, she had to figure Roarke knew what he was doing.

At the sound of the mixed voices rolling out of the ballroom as they approached, Eve shook her head. "I bet half of them are already in the bag. You're serving prime stuff in there, aren't you?"

"Only the best for our hardworking civil servants." Knowing his woman, Roarke took her hand and pulled her through the open doorway.

The ballroom was huge, and packed. They'd come from all over the planet, and its satellites. Police officials, technicians, expert consultants. The brains and the brawn of law enforcement.

"Doesn't it make you nervous to be in the same room with, what, about four thousand cops?" she asked him.

"On the contrary, Lieutenant," he said laughingly. "I feel very safe."

"Some of these guys probably tried to put you away once upon a time."

"So did you." Now he took her hand and, before she could stop him, kissed it. "Look where it got you."

"Dallas!" Officer Delia Peabody, decked out in a short red dress instead of her standard starched uniform, rushed up. Her dark bowl of hair had been fluffed and curled. And, Eve noted, the tall glass in her hand was already half empty.

"Peabody. Looks like you got here."

"The transport was on time, no problem. Roarke, this place is seriously iced. I can't believe I'm here. I really appreciate you getting me in, Dallas."

She hadn't arranged it as a favor, exactly. If she was going to suffer through a seminar, Eve had figured her aide should suffer, too. But from the look of things Peabody seemed to be bearing up.

"I came in with Feeney and his wife," Peabody went on. "And Dr. Mira and her husband. Morris and Dickhead and Silas from Security, Leward from Anti-Crime—they're all around somewhere. Some of the other guys from Central and the precincts. NYPSD is really well represented."

"Great." She could expect to get ragged on about her speech for weeks.

"We're going to have a little reunion later in the Moon-scape Lounge."

"Reunion? We just saw each other yesterday."

"On-planet." Peabody's lips, slicked deep red, threatened to pout. "This is different."

Eve scowled at her aide's fancy party dress. "You're telling me."

"Why don't I get you ladies a drink? Wine, Eve? And Peabody?"

"I'm having an Awesome Orgasm. The drink, I mean, not, you know, personally."

Amused, Roarke brushed a hand over her shoulder. "I'll take care of it."

"Boy, could he ever," Peabody muttered as he walked away.

"Button it." Eve scanned the room, separating cops from spouses, from techs, from consultants. She focused in on a large group gathered in the southeast corner of the ballroom. "What's the deal there?"

"That's the big wheel. Former Commander Douglas R. Skinner." Peabody gestured with her glass, then took a long drink. "You ever meet him?"

"No. Heard about him plenty, though."

"He's a legend. I haven't gotten a look yet because there's been about a hundred people around him since I got here. I've read most of his books. The way he came through the Urban Wars, kept his own turf secure. He was wounded dur-ing the Atlanta Siege, but held the line. He's a real hero."

"Cops aren't heroes, Peabody. We just do the job."

2

Eve wasn't interested in legends or heroes or retired cops who raked in enormous fees playing the lecture circuit or consulting. She was interested in finishing her one drink, putting in an appearance at the reception—and only because her own commander had ordered her to do so—then making herself scarce.

Tomorrow, she thought, was soon enough to get down to work. From the noise level of the crowd, everyone else thought so, too.

But it appeared the legend was interested in her.

She barely had the wineglass in her hand, was just calculating the least annoying route around the room, when someone tapped on her shoulder.

"Lieutenant Dallas." A thin man with dark hair cut so short it looked like sandpaper glued to his scalp, nodded at her. "Bryson Hayes, Commander Skinner's personal adjutant. The commander would very much like to meet you. If you'd come with me."

"The commander," she returned even as Hayes started to turn away, "looks pretty occupied at the moment. I'll be around all week."

After one slow blink, Hayes simply stared at her. "The commander would like to meet you now, Lieutenant. His schedule through the conference is very demanding."

"Go on." Peabody whispered it as she nudged Eve with her elbow. "Go on, Dallas."

"We'd be delighted to meet with Commander Skinner." Roarke solved the problem by setting his own drink aside, then taking both Eve's and Peabody's arms. It earned him an adoring-puppy look from Peabody and a narrow scowl from his wife.

Before Hayes could object or adjust, Roarke led both women across the ballroom.

"You're just doing this to piss me off," Eve commented.

"Not entirely, but I did enjoy pissing Hayes off. Just a bit of politics, Lieutenant." He gave her arm a friendly squeeze. "It never hurts to play them."

He slipped through the crowd smoothly, and only smiled when Hayes, a muscle working in his jaw, caught up in time to break a path through the last knot of people.

Skinner was short. His reputation was so large, it surprised Eve to note that he barely reached her shoulders. She knew him to be seventy, but he'd kept himself in shape. His face was lined, but it didn't sag. Nor did his body. He'd allowed his hair to gray, but not to thin, and he wore it militarily trim. His eyes, under straight silver brows, were a hard marble blue.

He held a short glass, the amber liquid inside neat. The heavy gold of his fifty-year ring gleamed on his finger.

She took his measure in a matter of seconds as, she noted, he took hers.

"Lieutenant Dallas."

"Commander Skinner." She accepted the hand he held out, found it cool, dry and more frail than she'd expected. "My aide, Officer Peabody."

His gaze stayed on Eve's face an extra beat, then shifted to Peabody. His lips curved. "Officer, always a pleasure to meet one of our men or women in uniform."

"Thank you, sir. It's an honor to meet you, Commander. You're one of the reasons I joined the force."

"I'm sure the NYPSD is lucky to have you. Lieutenant, I'd—"

"My husband," Eve interrupted. "Roarke."

Skinner's expression didn't waver, but it chilled. "Yes, I

recognized Roarke. I spent some of my last decade on the job studying you."

"I'm flattered. I believe this is your wife." Roarke turned his attention to the woman beside Skinner. "It's a pleasure to meet you."

"Thank you." Her voice was the soft cream of the southern United States. "Your Olympus is a spectacular accomplishment. I'm looking forward to seeing more of it while we're here."

"I'd be happy to arrange a tour, transportation."

"You're too kind." She brushed a hand lightly over her husband's arm.

She was a striking woman. She had to be close to her husband in age, Eve thought, as their long marriage was part of Skinner's pristine rep. But either superior DNA or an excellent face-and-body team had kept her beauty youthful. Her hair was richly black, and the gorgeous tone of her skin indicated mixed race. She wore a sleek silver gown and starry diamonds as if she'd been born to such things.

When she looked at Eve it was with polite interest. "My husband admires your work, Lieutenant Dallas, and he's very exacting in his admiration. Roarke, why don't we give these two cops a little time to talk shop?"

"Thank you, Belle. Excuse us, won't you, Officer?" Skinner gestured toward a table guarded by a trio of black-suited men. "Lieutenant? Indulge me." When they sat, the men moved one step back.

"Bodyguards at a cop convention?"

"Habit. I wager you have your weapon and shield in your evening bag."

She acknowledged this with a little nod. She would have preferred to wear them, but the dress didn't allow for her choice of accessories. "What's this about, Commander?"

"Belle was right. I admire your work. I was intrigued to find us on the same program. You don't generally accept speaking engagements."

"No. I like the streets."

"So did I. It's like a virus in the blood." He leaned back, nursed his drink. The faint tremor in his hand surprised her. "But working the streets doesn't mean being on them, necessarily. Someone has to command—from a desk, an office, a war room. A good cop, a smart cop, moves up the ranks. As you have, Lieutenant."

"A good cop, a smart cop, closes cases and locks up the bad guys."

He gave one short laugh. "You think that's enough for captain's bars, for a command star? No, the word 'naive' never came up in any of the reports I've read on you."

"Why should you read reports on me?"

"I may be retired from active duty, but I'm still a consultant. I still have my finger in the pie." He leaned forward again. "You've managed to work and close some very high-profile cases in the murder book, Lieutenant. While I don't always approve of your methods, the results are unarguable. It's rare for me to judge a female officer worthy of command."

"Excuse me. Back up. Female?"

He lifted his hand in a gesture that told her he'd had this discussion before and was vaguely weary of it. "I believe men and women have different primary functions. Man is the warrior, the provider, the defender. Woman is the procreator, the nurturer. There are numerous scientific theories that agree, and certainly social and religious weight to add."

"Is that so?" Eve said softly.

"Frankly, I've never approved of women on the force, or in certain areas of the civilian workplace. They're often a distraction and rarely fully committed to the job. Marriage and family soon—as they should for women—take priority."

"Commander Skinner, under the circumstances, the most courteous thing I can think of to say is you're full of shit."

He laughed, loud and long. "You live up to your reputation, Lieutenant. Your data also indicate that you're smart and that your badge isn't something you just pick up off the dresser every morning. It's what you are. Or were, in any case. We have that in common. For fifty years I made a difference, and my house was clean. I did what had to be done, then I did what came next. I was full commander at the age of forty-four. Would you like to be able to say the same?"

She knew when she was being played, and kept her face and tone neutral. "I haven't thought about it."

"If that's true, you disappoint me. If that's true, start thinking. Do you know, Lieutenant, how much closer you would be right now to a captaincy if you hadn't made some ill-advised personal decisions?"

"Really?" Something began to burn inside her gut. "And how would you know the promotion potential of a homicide cop in New York?"

"I've made it my business to know." His free hand balled into a fist, tapped lightly, rhythmically on the tabletop. "I have one regret, one piece of unfinished business from my active duty. One target I could never keep in my sights long enough to bring down. Between us, we could. I'll get you those captain bars, Lieutenant. You get me Roarke."

She looked down at her wine, slowly ran a fingertip around the rim. "Commander, you gave half a century of your life to the job. You shed blood for it. That's the single reason I'm not going to punch you in the face for that insult."

"Think carefully," he said as Eve got to her feet. "Sentiment over duty is never a smart choice. I intend to bring him down. I won't hesitate to break you to do it."

Riding on fury, she leaned down very close, and whispered in his ear. "Try it. You'll find out I'm no fucking nurturer."

She stepped away, only to have one of the bodyguards move into her path. "The commander," he said, "isn't finished speaking with you."

"I'm finished speaking with the commander."

His gaze shifted from her face briefly, and he gave the faintest nod before he edged closer, clamped a hand on her arm. "You'll want to sit down, Lieutenant, and wait until you've been dismissed."

"Move your hand. Move it now, or I'm going to hurt you."

He only tightened his grip. "Take your seat and wait for leave to go. Or you're going to be hurt."

She glanced back at Skinner, then into the guard's face. "Guess again." She used a short-arm jab to break his nose, then a quick snap kick to knock back the guard beside him as he surged forward.

By the time she'd spun around, planted, she had her hand in her bag and on her weapon. "Keep your dogs on a leash," she said to Skinner.

She scanned the faces of cops who'd turned, who'd moved forward, to see if there was trouble coming from another direction. Deciding against it, she turned away and walked through the buzzing crowd.

She was nearly at the door when Roarke fell in step beside her, draped an arm around her shoulders. "You got blood on your dress, darling."

"Yeah?" Still steaming, she glanced down at the small splatter. "It's not mine."

"I noticed."

"I need to talk to you."

"Um-hmm. Why don't we go upstairs, see what the valet can do about that bloodstain? You can talk before we come down to have a drink with your friends from Central."

"Why the hell didn't you tell me you knew Skinner?"

Roarke keyed in the code for the private elevator to the owner's suite. "I don't know him."

"He sure as hell knows you."

"So I gathered." He waited until they were inside the car before he pressed a kiss to her temple. "Eve, over the course of things, I've had a great many cops looking in my direction."

"He's still looking."

"He's welcome to. I'm a legitimate businessman. Practically a pillar. Redeemed by the love of a good woman."

"Don't make me hit you, too." She strode out of the elevator, across the sumptuous living area of the suite, and directly outside onto the terrace so she could finish steaming in fresh air. "The son of a bitch. The son of a bitch wants me to help him bring you down."

"Rather rude," Roarke said mildly. "To broach the subject on such a short acquaintance, and at a cocktail reception. Why did he think you'd agree?"

"He dangled a captaincy in my face. Tells me he can get it for me, otherwise I'm in the back of the line because of my poor personal choices."

"Meaning me." Amusement fled. "Is that true? Are your chances for promotion bogged down because of us?"

"How the hell do I know?" Still flying on the insult, she rounded on him. "Do you think I care about that? You think making rank drives me?"

"No." He walked to her, ran his hands up and down her arms. "I know what drives you. The dead drive you." He leaned forward, rested his lips on her brow. "He miscalculated."

"It was a stupid and senseless thing for him to do. He barely bothered to circle around much before he hit me with it. Bad strategy," she continued. "Poor approach. He wants your ass, Roarke, and bad enough to risk censure for attempted bribery if I report the conversation—and anyone believes it. Why is that?"

"I don't know." And what you didn't know, he thought, was always dangerous. "I'll look into it. In any case, you certainly livened up the reception."

"Normally I'd've been more subtle, just kneed that jerk in the balls for getting in my way. But Skinner had gone into this tango about how women shouldn't be on the job because they're nurturers. Tagging the balls just seemed too girly at the time."

He laughed, drew her closer. "I love you, Eve."

"Yeah, yeah." But she was smiling again when she wrapped her arms around him.

As a rule, being crowded ass to ass at a table in a club where the entertainment included music that threatened the eardrums wasn't Eve's idea of a good time.

But when she was working off a good mad, it paid to have friends around.

The table was jammed with New York's finest. Her butt was squeezed between Roarke's and Feeney's, the Electronic Detective Division captain. Feeney's usually hangdog face was slack with amazement as he stared up at the stage.

On the other side of Roarke, Dr. Mira, elegant despite the surroundings, sipped a Brandy Alexander and watched the entertainment—a three-piece combo whose costumes were red-white-and-blue body paint doing wild, trash-rock riffs on American folk songs. Rounding out the table were Morris, the medical examiner, and Peabody.

"Wife shouldn't've gone to bed." Feeney shook his head. "You have to see it to believe it."

"Hell of a show," Morris agreed. His long, dark braid was threaded through with silver rope, and the lapels of his calf-length jacket sparkled with the same sheen.

For a dead doctor, Eve thought, he was a very snappy dresser.

"But Dallas here"—Morris winked at her—"was quite some warm-up act."

"Har har," Eve replied.

Morris smiled serenely. "Hotshot lieutenant decks legend of police lore's bodyguards at law enforcement convention on luxury off-planet resort. You've got to play that all the way out."

"Nice left jab," Feeney commented. "Good follow-through on the kick. Skinner's an asshole."

"Why do you say that, Feeney?" Peabody demanded. "He's an icon."

"Who said icons can't be assholes?" he tossed back. "Likes to make out like he put down the Urban Wars single-handed. Goes around talking about them like it was all about duty and romance and patriotism. What it was, was about survival. And it was ugly."

"It's typical for some who've been through combat to romanticize it," Mira put in.

"Nothing romantic about slitting throats or seeing Fifth Avenue littered with body parts."

"Well, that's cheerful." Morris pushed Feeney's fresh glass in front of him. "Have another beer, Captain."

"Cops don't crow about doing the job." Feeney glugged down his beer. "They just do it. I'da been closer, Dallas, I'da helped you take down those spine crackers of his."

Because the wine and his mood made her sentimental, she jabbed him affectionately with her elbow. "You bet your ass. We can go find them and beat them brainless. You know, round out the evening's entertainment."

Roarke laid a hand on her back as one of his security people came to the table and leaned down to whisper in his ear. Humor vanished from his face as he nodded.

"Someone beat you to it," he announced. "We have what's left of a body on the stairway between the eighteenth and nineteenth floors."

3

Eve stood at the top of the stairwell. The once pristine white walls were splattered with blood and gray matter. A nasty trail of both smeared the stairs. The body was sprawled on them, faceup.

There was enough of his face and hair left for her to identify him as the man whose nose she'd broken a few hours before.

"Looks like somebody was a lot more pissed off than I was. Your man got any Seal-It?" she asked Roarke.

When Roarke passed her the small can of sealant, she coated her hands, her shoes. "I could use a recorder. Peabody, help hotel security keep the stairwells blocked off. Morris." She tossed him the can. "With me."

Roarke gave her his security guard's lapel recorder. Stepped forward. Eve simply put a hand on his chest. "No civilians—whether they own the hotel or not. Just wait. Why don't you clear Feeney to confiscate the security disks for this sector of the hotel? It'll save time."

She didn't wait for an answer, but headed down the steps to the body. Crouched. "Didn't do this with fists." She examined his face. One side was nearly caved in, the other largely untouched. "Left arm's crushed. Guy was left-handed. I made that at the reception. They probably went for the left side first. Disabled him."

"Agreed. Dallas?" Morris jerked his head in the direction of the seventeenth floor. A thick metal bat coated with gore rested on a tread farther down the stairs. "That would've done the trick. I can consult with the local ME on the autopsy, but prelim eyeballing tells me that's the weapon. Do you want me to dig up some evidence bags, a couple of field kits?"

She started to speak, then hissed out a breath. The smell of death was in her nostrils, and it was too familiar. "Not our territory. We've got to go through station police. Goddamn it."

"There are ways to get around that, with your man owning the place."

"Maybe." She poked a sealed finger in a blood pool, nudged something metal and silver. And she recognized the star worn on the epaulets of hotel security.

"Who would be stupid enough to beat a man to death in a hotel full of cops?" Morris wondered.

She shook her head, got to her feet. "Let's get the ball rolling on this." When she reached the top of the steps, she scanned the hallway. If she'd been in New York, she would now give the body a thorough examination, establish time of death, gather data and trace evidence from the scene. She'd call her crime scene unit, the sweepers, and send out a team to do door-to-doors.

But she wasn't in New York.

"Has your security notified station police?" she asked Roarke.

"They're on their way."

"Good. Fine. We'll keep the area secure and offer any and all assistance." Deliberately, she switched off her recorder. "I don't have any authority here. Technically, I shouldn't have entered the crime scene area. I had a previous altercation with the victim, and that makes it stickier."

"I own this hotel, and I hold primary interest in this station. I can request the assistance of any law enforcement agent."

"Yeah, so we've got that clear." She looked at him. "One of your security uniforms is missing a star. It's down there, covered with body fluid."

"If one of my people is responsible, you'll have my full cooperation in identifying and apprehending him."

She nodded again. "So we've got that clear, too. What's your security setup for this sector?"

"Full-range cameras—corridors, elevators, and stairwells. Full soundproofing. Feeney's getting the disks."

"He'll have to hand them to station police. When it's homicide, they have a maximum of seventy-two hours before they're obliged to turn the investigation over to ILE. Since ILE has people on-site, they'd be wise to turn it over now."

"Is that what you want?"

"It's not a matter of what I want. Look, it's not my case."

He took a handkerchief out of his pocket and wiped the blood smear from her hand. "Isn't it?"

Then he turned as the chief of police stepped off the elevator.

Eve hadn't been expecting a statuesque brunette in a tiny black dress with enough hair to stuff a mattress. As she clipped down the hall on towering high heels, Eve heard Morris's reverent opinion.

"Hubba-hubba."

"Jeez, try for dignity," Eve scolded.

The brunette stopped, took a quick scan. "Roarke," she said in a voice that evoked images of hot desert nights.

"Chief. Lieutenant Dallas, NYPSD. Dr. Morris, NYC Medical Examiner."

"Yes. Darcia Angelo. Chief of Olympus Police. Excuse my appearance. I was at one of the welcome events. I'm told we have a possible homicide."

"Verified homicide," Eve told her. "Victim's male, Caucasian, thirty-five to forty. Bludgeoned. The weapon, a metal bat, was left on scene. Preliminary visual exam indicates he's been dead under two hours."

"There's been a prelim exam?" Darcia asked. Coldly.

"Yes."

"Well, we won't quibble about that. I'll verify personally before my team gets here."

"Messy down there." Coolly, Eve handed over the can of Seal-It.

"Thanks." Darcia stepped out of her evening shoes. Eve couldn't fault her for it. She did the same thing herself, when she remembered. When she'd finished, she handed the can back to Eve. Darcia took a small recorder out of her purse, clipped it where the fabric of her dress dipped to hug her breasts.

Morris let out a long sigh as she walked into the stairwell. "Where do you find them?" he asked Roarke. "And how can I get one of my very own?"

Before Eve could snarl at him, Feeney hurried down the hall. "Got a snag with the disks," he announced. "Stairway cams were overridden for a fifty-minute period. You got nothing but static there, and static for two sixty-second intervals on the twentieth-floor corridor. Somebody knew what they were doing," he added. "It's a complex system, with a fail-safe backup plan. It took a pro—with access."

"With that time frame there had to be at least two people involved," Eve stated. "Premeditated, not impulse, not crime of passion."

"You got an ID on the victim? I can run a background check."

"Police chief's on scene," Eve said flatly.

For a moment Feeney looked blank. "Oh, right. Forgot we weren't home, sweet home. The locals going to squeeze us out?"

"You weren't," Darcia said as she came out of the stairwell, "ever—in an official capacity—in."

"On the contrary," Roarke told her. "I requested the assistance of the lieutenant and her team."

Irritation flickered across Darcia's face, but she controlled it quickly. "As is your privilege. Lieutenant, may I have a moment of your time?" Without waiting for an answer, Darcia walked down the corridor.

"Arrogant, territorial, pushy." Eve glared at Roarke. "You sure can pick them."

He only smiled as his wife's retreating back. "Yes, I certainly can."

"Look, Angelo, you want to bust my balls over doing a visual, you're wasting your time and mine." Eve tugged her lapel recorder free, held it out. "I verified a homicide, at the request of the property owner. Then I stepped back. I don't want your job, and I don't want your case. I get my fill of walking through blood in New York."

Darcia flipped her mane of glossy black hair. "Four months ago I was busting illegal dealers in Colombia, risking my life on a daily basis and still barely able to pay the rent on a stinking little two-room apartment. In the current climate, cops are not appreciated in my country. I like my new job."

She opened her purse, dropped Eve's recorder inside. "Is that job in jeopardy if I refuse to hand over this case to my employer's wife?"

"Roarke doesn't fight my battles, and he doesn't fire people because they might not agree with me."

"Good." Darcia nodded. "I worked illegals, bunko, robbery. Twelve years. I'm a good cop. Homicide, however, is not my specialty. I don't enjoy sharing, but I'd appreciate any help you and your associates are willing to give in this matter."

"Fine. So what was this dance about?"

"Simply? So you and I would both be aware it *is* my case."

"You need to be aware that earlier tonight I punched the dead man in the face."

"Why?" Darcia asked suspiciously.

"He got in my way."

"I see. It'll be interesting to find out if you and I can close this matter without getting in each other's way."

Two hours later, for convenience's sake, the two arms of the investigation gathered in Roarke's on-site office.

"The victim is identified as Reginald Weeks, thirty-eight. Current residence is Atlanta, Georgia, Earth. Married, no children. Current employer, Douglas R. Skinner, Incorporated. Function, personal security." Darcia finished, inclined her head at Eve.

"Crime scene examination of body shows massive trauma." Eve picked up the narrative. "Cause of death, most likely, fractured skull. The left side of the head and body were severely traumatized. Victim was left-handed, and this method of attack indicates foreknowledge. Security for the stairwell and the twentieth floor were tampered with prior to and during the act. A metal bat has been taken into evidence and is presumed to be the murder weapon. Also taken into evidence a silver-plated star stud, identified as part of the hotel security team's uniform. Chief Angelo?"

"Background data so far retrieved on Weeks show no criminal activity. He had held his current employment for two years. Prior that, he was employed by Right Arm, a firm that handles personal security and security consults for members of the Conservative Party. Prior to that he was in the military, Border Patrol, for six years."

"This tells us he knows how to follow orders," Eve continued. "He stepped up in my face tonight because Skinner, or one of Skinner's arms, signaled him to do so. He laid hands on me for the same reason. He's trained, and if he was good enough to last six years in the Border Patrol and land a job in Right Arm, he's not the type of guy who would go into a soundproof stairwell with a stranger, even under duress. If he'd been attacked in the corridor, there'd be a sign of it. If they took him on the twentieth floor, what the hell was he doing on the twentieth floor? His room, his security briefing room, and Skinner's suite are all on twenty-six."

"Could've been meeting a woman." Feeney stretched out his legs. "Conventionitis."

"That's a point," Eve allowed. "All evidence points to this being a planned attack, but a woman could have been used as a lure. We need to verify or eliminate that. You want to track it down, Feeney?"

"Captain Feeney may assist my officers in that area of investigation." Darcia merely lifted her eyebrows when Eve turned to her. "If he is agreeable. As I hope he will be to continuing to work with the hotel security team."

"We're a real agreeable group," Eve said with a wide, wide smile.

"Excellent. Then you have no problem accompanying me to twenty-six to inform the victim's employer of his death."

"Not a one. Peabody. My aide goes with me," Eve said before Darcia could speak. "Non-negotiable. Peabody," Eve said again, gesturing as she walked out of the room and left Darcia assigning her officers to different tasks. "I want your recorder on when we talk to Skinner."

"Yes, sir."

"If I get hung up, I need you to wheedle an update out of the local ME. If you can't open him up, tag Morris and have him use the good buddy, same field approach."

"Yes, sir."

"I want to find the uniform that star came from. We need to check recyclers, the valet, outside cleaning sources. Get chummy with the home team. I want to know the minute the sweepers and crime scene units reports are in. I'm betting there's going to be traces of Seal-It on that bat, and nobody's blood but the victim's on the scene. Fucking ambush," she grumbled, and turned as Darcia came out.

Darcia said nothing until she'd called for the elevator and stepped inside. "Do you have a history with Douglas Skinner, Lieutenant?"

"No. Not until tonight."

"My information is that he specifically called you to his table to speak with you privately. You, apparently, had words of disagreement, and when the victim attempted to prevent you from leaving the table, you struck him. Would this be accurate?"

"It would."

"What were those words of disagreement between you and Douglas Skinner?"

"Am I a suspect in this case or a consultant?"

"You're a consultant, and as such I would appreciate any and all data."

"I'll think about it." Eve stepped out on twenty-six.

"If you have nothing to hide."

"I'm a cop," Eve reminded her. "That line doesn't work on me." She rang the bell, waited. She watched the security light blink to green, kept her face blank while she and her companions were scanned. Moments later, Skinner opened the door himself.

"Lieutenant. It's a bit late for paying calls."

"It's never too late for official calls. Chief Angelo, Douglas Skinner."

"Pardon the intrusion, Commander Skinner." Darcia's voice was low and respectful, her face quietly sober. "We have some unfortunate news. May we come in?"

"Of course." He stepped back. He was dressed in the long white robe provided by the hotel, and his face looked pale against it. The large living area was dimly lit and fragrant from the bouquets of roses. He ordered the lights up 10 percent, and gestured toward the sofa.

"Please, ladies, sit. Can I get you anything? Coffee, perhaps?"

"We're not here to chat. Where were you between twenty-two hundred and midnight?"

"I don't like your tone, Lieutenant."

"Please, excuse us." Darcia stepped in smoothly. "It's been a difficult night. If I could ask you to verify your whereabouts, as a formality?"

"My wife and I came up to our suite a bit after ten. We retired early, as I have a long, busy day scheduled tomorrow. What's happened?"

"Weeks got his brains bashed in," Eve said.

"Weeks? Reggie?" Skinner stared at Eve. Those hard blue eyes widened, darkened, and seemed to draw a cast of gray over his skin as shock shifted into fury. "Dead? The boy is dead? Have you determined Roarke's *whereabouts*? Or would you go so far as to cover up murder to protect him? She attacked Weeks only hours ago." He pointed at Eve. "An unprovoked and vicious assault on one of mine because I questioned her about her alliance with a criminal. You're a disgrace to your badge."

"One of us is," Eve agreed as Skinner sank into a chair.

"Commander." Darcia stepped forward. "I know this is a shock for you. I want to assure you that the Olympus PD is actively pursuing all avenues of investigation."

For a moment he said nothing, and the only sound was his quick, labored breathing. "I don't know you, Chief Angelo, but I know who pays you. I have no confidence in your investigation as long as it's bankrolled by Roarke. Now, excuse me. I have nothing more to say at this time. I need to contact Reggie's wife and tell her she's a widow."

4

"*Well, that went well.*" *Eve rolled her shoulders as she* headed back to the elevator.

"If one doesn't mind being accused of being a fool or a dirty cop."

Eve punched the elevator button. "Ever hear the one about sticks and stones in Colombia?"

"I don't like that one." Obviously stewing, Darcia strode onto the elevator. "And I don't like your Commander Skinner."

"Hey, he's not mine."

"He implied Roarke is my puppet master. Why does he assume that, and why does he believe Roarke is responsible for Weeks's death?"

The quiet, respectful woman was gone, and in her place was a tough-eyed cop with steel in her voice. Eve began to see how Darcia Angelo had risen through twelve years in Colombia.

"One reason is Weeks annoyed me, and since I'm just a procreating, nurturing female, it would be up to my warrior, defender, penis-owning husband to follow through."

"Ah." Darcia sucked in her cheeks. "This is an attitude I recognize. Still, splattering a man's brains is considerable overcompensation for such a minor infraction. A very large leap of conclusion for the commander to make. There's more."

"Might be. I haven't worked it out yet. Meanwhile, Skinner seemed awfully alert for someone who'd already gone to bed. And while the lights in the living area were on low when we walked in, they were full on in the bedroom off to the right. He didn't close the door all the way when he came out."

"Yes, I noticed that."

"Suite's set up along the same basic floor plan as the one I'm in. Second bedroom off to the left. There was a light on in there, too. His wife had that door open a crack. She was listening."

"I didn't catch that," Darcia mused, then glanced back when Peabody muttered.

"She missed it, too," Eve said. "She hates that. And if Belle Skinner was eavesdropping from the second bedroom, she wasn't snuggled up with the commander in the master, was she? No connubial bliss, which is interesting. And no alibi."

"What motive would Skinner have for killing one of his own bodyguards?"

"Something to think about. I want to check some things out." She stopped the elevator so both Darcia and Peabody could exit. "I'll get back to you."

Being willing to fall into step with Darcia Angelo didn't mean she couldn't make some lateral moves of her own. If she was going to wade into a murder investigation off her own turf, without her usual system and when her badge was little more than a fashion accessory, she was going to make use of whatever tools were available.

There was one particular tool she knew to be very versatile and flexible.

She was married to him.

She found Roarke, as she'd expected to, at work on the bedroom computer. He'd removed his dinner jacket, rolled up his sleeves. There was a pot of coffee beside him.

"What have you got?" She picked up his cup, gulped down half his coffee.

"Nothing that links me or any of my business dealings with Skinner. I have some interests in Atlanta, naturally."

"Naturally."

"Communications, electronics, entertainment. Real estate, of course." He took the cup back from her, idly rubbed her ass with his free hand. "And during one lovely interlude previous to my association with you, a nicely profitable smuggling enterprise. Federal infractions—"

"Infractions," she repeated.

"One could say. Nothing that bumped up against state or local authorities."

"Then you're missing something, because it's personal with him. It doesn't make any sense otherwise. You're not a major bad guy."

"Now you've hurt my feelings."

"Why does he latch on to you?" she demanded, ignoring him. "Fifty years a cop, he'd have seen it all. And he'd have lost plenty. There are stone killers out there, pedophiles, sexual predators, cannibals, for Christ's sake. So why are you stuck in his craw? He's been retired from active, what, six years, and—"

"Seven."

"Seven, then. Seven years. And he approaches me with what could be considered a bribe or blackmail, depending on your point of view, to pressure me into rolling over on you. It was arrogant and ill-conceived."

She thought it through as she paced. "I don't think he expected it to work. I think he expected me to tell him to fuck off. That way he could roll us into a ball together and shoot two for one."

"He can't touch you—or me, for that matter."

"He can make things hot by implicating us in a homicide. And he's laying the groundwork. He pushes my buttons in a public venue, then gets one of his monkeys to get in my face. Altercation ensues. A couple hours later, monkey has his brains splattered all over the stairway of a Roarke Enterprises hotel—and what's this! Why it's a clue, Sherlock, and a dandy one, too. A star stud from one of Roarke Securities uniforms, floating in the victim's blood."

"Not particularly subtle."

"He doesn't have time to be subtle. He's in a hurry," she continued. "I don't know why, but he's rushing things. Shove circumstantial evidence down the throat of the local authorities and they've got to pursue the possibility that the irritated husband and suspected interplanetary hoodlum ordered one of his own monkeys to teach Skinner's a lesson."

"You touched my wife, now I have to kill you?" Roarke's shrug was elegant and careless. "Overdramatic, over-romanticized. Particularly since you punched him in the face before I could ride to the rescue."

"In his narrow little world, men are the hunters, the defenders. It plays when you look at it through his window. It's another miscalculation though, because it's not your style. You want the hell beat out of someone, you do it yourself."

He smiled at her fondly. "I like watching you do it even more, darling."

She spared him a look. "Standard testing on you, any profile would kick the theory out of the park. You're just not hardwired to pay somebody to kill, or to get your dick in a twist because somebody hassles me. We could have Mira run you through a Level One testing just to push that aside."

"No, thank you, darling. More coffee?"

She grunted, paced a bit more while he rose to go to the mini AutoChef for a fresh pot and cups. "It's a sloppy frame. Thing is, Skinner believes you're capable, and that if he dumps enough on the ILE if and when they take over he'll push you into an investigative process that will mess you up—and me by association."

"Lieutenant, the ILE has investigated me in the past. They don't worry me. What does is that if it goes that far, your reputation and career could take some bruises. I won't tolerate that. I think the commander and I should have a chat."

"And what do you think he's counting on?" she demanded.

"Why disappoint him?" Coffee cup in hand, he sat on the arm of his chair. "I've compiled personal and professional data on Skinner. Nothing seems particularly relevant to this, but I haven't studied his case files in depth. Yet."

Eve set down the coffee he'd just poured her with a little snap of china on wood. "Case files? You hacked into his case files? Are you a lunatic? He gets wind of that, you're up on charges and in lockup before your fancy lawyers can knot their fancy ties."

"He won't get wind of it."

"CompuGuard—" She broke off, scowled at the bedroom unit. CompuGuard monitored all e-transmissions and programming on-planet or off. Though she was aware Roarke had unregistered equipment at home, the hotel system was a different matter. "Are you telling me this unit's unregistered?"

"Absolutely not." His expression was innocent as a choirboy's. "It's duly registered and meets all legal requirements. Or did until a couple of hours ago."

"You can't filter out CompuGuard in a few hours."

Roarke sighed heavily, shook his head. "First you hurt my feelings, now you insult me. I don't know why I put up with this abuse."

Then he moved fast, grabbing her up, hauling her against him and crushing her mouth with a kiss so hot she wondered if her lips were smoking.

"Oh, yes." He released her, picked up his coffee again. "That's why."

"If that was supposed to distract me from the fact that you've illegally blocked CompuGuard and broken into official data, it was a damn good try. But the joke's on you. I was going to ask you to dig up the data."

"Were you really, Lieutenant? You never fail to surprise me."

"They beat him until his bones were dust." Her tone was flat, dull. All cop. "They erased half his face. And left the other half clean so I'd know as soon as I saw him. The minute he stepped in front of me tonight, he was dead. I was the goddamn murder weapon." She looked back at the computer. "So. Let's get to work."

They culled out cases during Skinner's last decade of active duty and cross-referenced with anything relating to them during the seven years of his retirement. It overlapped the time before Roarke had come to America from Ireland, but it seemed a logical place to start.

As the caseload was enormous, they split it. Eve worked on the bedroom unit, and Roarke set up in the second bedroom.

By three, Eve's temples were throbbing, her stomach raw

from caffeine intake. And she'd developed a new and reluctant admiration for Commander Skinner.

"Damn good cop," she acknowledged. Thorough, focused, and up until his retirement, he had apparently dedicated himself, body and soul, to the job.

How had it felt to step away from all that? she wondered. It had been his choice, after all. At sixty-four, retirement was an option, not a requirement. He could have easily put in another ten years on active. He might have risen to commissioner.

Instead, he'd put in his fifty and then used that as a springboard in a run for Congress. And had fallen hard on his face. A half century of public service hadn't been enough to offset views so narrow even the most dug-in of the Conservative Party had balked. Added to that, his platform had swung unevenly from side to side.

He was an unwavering supporter of the Gun Ban, something the Conservatives tried to overturn at every opportunity. Yet he beat the drum to reinstate the death penalty, which alienated the Liberals from mid-road to far left.

He wanted to dissolve legal and regulated prostitution and strike out all legal and tax benefits for cohabitating couples. He preached about the sanctity of marriage, as long as it was heterosexual, but disavowed the government stipend for professional mothers.

Motherhood, the gospel according to Skinner stated, was a God-given duty, and payment in its own right.

His mixed-voice and muddled campaign had gone down in flames. However much he'd rebounded financially via lectures, books, and consults, Eve imagined he still bore the burns of that failure.

Still, she couldn't see how Roarke tied into it.

Rubbing her forehead, she pushed away and got up to work out the kinks. Maybe she was overreacting. Did she want it to be personal for Skinner because he'd made it personal for her? Maybe Roarke was no more than a symbol for Skinner. Someone who had slipped and slid around the system that Skinner himself had dedicated his life to.

She checked her wrist unit. Maybe she'd catch some sleep, go back to it fresh in the morning. She would juggle the data first, though, so that when she looked at it again it would be in a new pattern. Whatever she was missing—and her gut still told her she was missing something—might float to the top.

"Computer, extrapolate any and all references to Roarke . . ." She yawned hugely, shook her head to clear it. "In any and all files, personal and professional, under Skinner, Commander Douglas."

Working . . .

"List references chronologically, first to last, um . . . give me official police records first, followed by personal files."

Understood. Working. . . . No reference to Roarke under Skinner, Commander Douglas police records. Reference under Skinner, Captain Douglas only. . . . Extrapolating personal files . . .

"Yeah, well, you keep saying that, but . . ." Eve whirled around, stared at the monitor. "Computer, stop. List any and all reference to Roarke under Skinner, Douglas, any rank."

Working . . . first listed reference in Skinner, Captain Douglas, case file C-439014, to Roarke, Patrick a/k/a O'Hara, Sean, a/k/a MacNeil, Thomas, date stamped March, twelve, twenty-thirty-six. Subject Roarke suspect in illegal weapons running, illegal entry into United States, grand theft auto and conspiracy to murder of police officers. Subject believed to have fled Atlanta area, and subsequently the country. Last known residence, Dublin, Ireland. Case file complete, investigative data available. Do you wish full case file?

"Yes. In hard copy."

Working . . .

Eve sat down again, slowly as the computer hummed. 2036, she thought. Twenty-three years ago. Roarke would have been what, twelve, thirteen?

It wasn't Roarke that was at the root of Skinner's obsession.

It was Roarke's father.

At his own unit, Roarke ran through layers of Skinner's financials. Among the most clear-cut motives for murder were greed, revenge, jealousy, sex, fear of disgrace, and profit. So he'd follow the money first.

There was a possibility, he'd decided, that Skinner had invested in one of his companies—or a competitor's. Perhaps he'd lost a substantial amount of money. Men had hated men for less.

And financially Skinner had taken a beating during his run for Congress. It had left him nearly broke as well as humiliated.

"Roarke."

"Hmm." He held up a finger to hold Eve off as she came into the room. "Communications," he said. "I have an interest in the Atlanta media sources, and they were very unkind to Skinner during his congressional attempt. This would have weighed heavily against his chances of winning. Media Network Link is mine outright, and they were downright vicious. Accurate, but vicious. Added to that, he's invested fairly heavily in Corday Electronics, based in Atlanta. My own company has eroded their profits and customer base steadily for the last four years. I really should finish them off with a takeover," he added as an afterthought.

"Roarke."

"Yes?" He reached around absently to take her hand as he continued to scroll data.

"It goes deeper than politics and stock options. Twenty-three years ago illegal arms dealers set up a base in Atlanta, and Skinner headed up the special unit formed to take them down. They had a weasel on the inside, and solid information. But when they moved in, it was a trap. Weasels turn both ways, and we all know it."

She took a deep breath, hoping she was telling it the way it should be told. Love twisted her up as often, maybe more often, than it smoothed things out for her.

"Thirteen cops were killed," she continued, "six more wounded. They were outgunned, but despite it, Skinner broke the cartel's back. The cartel lost twenty-two men, mostly soldiers. And he bagged two of the top line that night. That led to two more arrests in the next twelve months. But he lost one. He was never able to get his hands on one."

"Darling, I might've been precocious, but at twelve I'd yet to run arms, unless you're counting a few hand-helds or homemade boomers sold in alleyways. And I hadn't ventured beyond Dublin City. As for weaseling, that's something I've never stooped to."

"No." She kept staring at his face. "Not you."

And watched his eyes change, darken and chill, as it fell into place for him. "Well, then," he said, very softly. "Son of a bitch."

5

As a boy, Roarke had been the favored recipient of his father's fists and boots. He'd usually seen them coming, and had avoided them when possible, lived with them when it wasn't.

To his knowledge, this was the first time the old man had sucker punched him from the grave.

Still, he sat calmly enough, reading the hard copy of the reports Eve had brought him. He was a long way from the skinny, battered boy who had run the Dublin alleyways. Though he didn't care much for having to remind himself of it now.

"This double cross went down a couple of months before my father ended up in the gutter with a knife in his throat. Apparently someone beat Skinner to him. He has that particular unsolved murder noted in his file here. Perhaps he arranged it."

"I don't think so." She wasn't quite sure how to approach Roarke on the subject of his father and his boyhood. He tended to walk away from his past, whereas she—well, she tended to walk into the wall of her own past no matter how often, how deliberately, she changed directions.

"Why do you say that? Look, Eve, it isn't the same for me as it is for you. You needn't be careful. He doesn't haunt me. Tell me why if my father slipped through Skinner's fingers in Atlanta, Skinner wouldn't arrange to have his throat slit in Dublin City."

"First, he was a cop, not an assassin. There's no record in the file that he'd located his target in Dublin. There's correspondence with Interpol, with local Irish authorities. He was working on extradition procedures should his target show up on Irish soil, and would likely have gotten the paperwork and the warrant. That's what he'd have wanted," she continued, and rose to prowl the room. "He'd want the bastard back on his own turf, back where it went down and his men were killed. He'd want that face-to-face. He didn't get it."

She turned back. "If he'd gotten it, he could've closed the book, moved on. And he wouldn't be compelled to go after you. You're what's left of the single biggest personal and professional failure of his life. He lost his men, and the person responsible for their loss got away from him."

"Dead wouldn't be enough, without arrest, trial, and sentencing."

"No, it wouldn't. And here you are, rich, successful, famous—and married, for Christ's sake—to a cop. I don't need Mira to draw me a profile on this one. Skinner believes that perpetrators of certain crimes, including any crime that results in the death of a police official, should pay with their life. After due process. Your father skipped out on that one. You're here, you pay."

"Then he's doomed to disappointment. For a number of reasons. One, I'm a great deal smarter than my father was." He rose, went to her, skimmed a finger down the dent in her chin. "And my cop is better than Skinner ever hoped to be."

"I have to take him down. I have to fuck over fifty years of duty, and take him down."

"I know." And would suffer for it, Roarke thought, as Skinner never would. As Skinner could never understand. "We need to sleep," he said and pressed his lips to her brow.

She dreamed of Dallas, and the frigid, filthy room in Texas where her father had kept her. She dreamed of cold and hunger and unspeakable fear. The red light from the sex club across the street flashed into the room, over her face. And over his face as he struck her.

She dreamed of pain when she dreamed of her father. The tearing of her young flesh as he forced himself into her. The snapping of bone, her own high, thin scream when he broke her arm.

She dreamed of blood.

Like Roarke's, her father had died by a knife. But the one that had killed him had been gripped in her own eight-year-old hand.

In the big, soft bed in the plush suite, she whimpered like a child. Beside her, Roarke gathered her close and held her until the dream died.

She was up and dressed by six. The snappy jacket that had ended up in her suitcase fit well over her harness and weapon. The weight of them made her feel more at home.

She used the bedroom 'link to contact Peabody. At least she assumed the lump under the heap of covers was Peabody.

"Whaa?"

"Wake up," Eve ordered. "I want your report in fifteen minutes."

"Who?"

"Jesus, Peabody. Get up, get dressed. Get here."

"Why don't I order up some breakfast?" Roarke suggested when she broke transmission.

"Fine, make it for a crowd. I'm going to spread a little sunshine and wake everybody up." She hesitated. "I trust my people, Roarke, and I know how much I can tell them. I don't know Angelo."

He continued to read the morning stock reports on-screen. "She works for me."

"So, one way or the other, does every third person in the known universe. That tells me nothing."

"What was your impression of her?"

"Sharp, smart, solid. And ambitious."

"So was mine," he said easily. "Or she wouldn't be chief of police on Olympus. Tell her what she needs to know. My father's unfortunate history doesn't trouble me."

"Will you talk to Mira?" She kept her gaze level as he

rose, turned toward her. "I want to call her in, I want a consult. Will you talk to her?"

"I don't need a therapist, Eve. I'm not the one with nightmares." He cursed softly, ran a hand through his hair when her face went blank and still. "Sorry. Bloody hell. But my point is we each handle things as we handle them."

"And you can push and nudge and find ways to smooth it over for me. But I can't do that for you."

The temper in her voice alleviated a large slice of his guilt over mentioning her nightmare. "Screen off," he ordered and crossed to her. Took her face in his hands. "Let me tell you what I once told Mira—not in a consult, not in a session. You saved me, Eve." He watched her blink in absolute shock. "What you are, what I feel for you, what we are together saved me." He kept his eyes on hers as he kissed her. "Call your people. I'll contact Darcia."

He was nearly out of the room before she found her voice. "Roarke?" She never seemed to find the words as he did, but these came easy. "We saved each other."

There was no way she could make the huge, elegant parlor feel like one of the conference rooms in Cop Central. Especially when her team was gorging on cream pastries, strawberries the size of golf balls, and a couple of pigs' worth of real bacon.

It just served to remind her how much she hated being off her own turf.

"Peabody, update."

Peabody had to jerk herself out of the image of the good angel on her shoulder, sitting with her hands properly folded, and the bad angel, who was stuffing another cream bun in her greedy mouth. "Ah, sir. Autopsy was completed last night. They let Morris assist. Cause of death multiple trauma, most specifically the skull fracture. A lot of the injuries were postmortem. He's booked on a panel this morning, and has some sort of dead doctors' seminar later today, but Morris will finesse copies of the reports for you. Early word is the tox screen was clear."

"Sweepers?" Eve demanded.

"Sweepers' reports weren't complete as of oh-six-hundred.

However, what I dug up confirmed your beliefs. Seal-It traces on the bat, no blood or bodily fluid but the victim's found on scene. No uniform missing an epaulet star has been found to date. Angelo's team's doing the run on recylers, valets, outside cleaning companies. My information is the uniforms are coded with the individual's ID number. When we find the uniform, we'll be able to trace the owner."

"I want that uniform," Eve stated, and when she turned to Feeney, the bad angel won. Peabody took another pastry.

"Had to be an inside job on the security cameras," he said. "Nobody gets access to Control without retina and palm scans and code clearance. The bypass was complicated, and it was done slick. Twelve people were in the control sector during the prime period last night. I'm running them."

"All right. We look for any connection to Skinner, any work-related reprimands, any sudden financial increase. Look twice if any of them were on the job before going into private security." She took a disk off the table, passed it to Feeney. "Run them with the names on here."

"No problem, but I work better when I know why I'm working."

"Those are the names of cops who went down in the line of duty in Atlanta twenty-three years ago. It was Skinner's operation." She took a deep breath. "Roarke's father was his weasel, and he turned a double cross."

When Feeney only nodded, Eve let out a breath. "One of the names on there is Thomas Weeks, father to Reginald Weeks, our victim. My guess is if Skinner had one of his slain officer's kids on his payroll, he's got others."

"Follows if one was used to build a frame around Roarke, another would be," Feeney added.

She checked her wrist unit when the door buzzer sounded. "That'll be Angelo. I want you running those names, Feeney, so I'm not giving them to her. Yet. But I'm going to tell her, and you, the rest of it."

While Eve was opening the door for Darcia, Skinner opened his to Roarke.

"A moment of your time, Commander."

"I have little to spare."

"Then we won't waste it." Roarke stepped inside, lifted a brow at Hayes. The man stood just behind and to the right of Skinner, and had his hand inside his suit jacket. "If you thought I was a threat, you should've had your man answer the door."

"You're no threat to me."

"Then why don't we have that moment in private?"

"Anything you say to me can be said in front of my personal assistant."

"Very well. It would've been tidier, and certainly more efficient, if you'd come after me directly instead of using Lieutenant Dallas and sacrificing one of your own men."

"So you admit you had him killed."

"I don't order death. We're alone, Skinner, and I'm sure you've had these rooms secured against recording devices and surveillance cameras. You want to take me on, then do it. But have the balls to leave my family out of it."

Skinner's lips peeled back over his teeth. "Your father was a dickless coward and a pathetic drunk."

"Duly noted." Roarke walked to a chair, sat. "There, you see. We already have a point of agreement on that particular matter. First let me clarify that by 'family,' I meant my wife. Second, I must tell you you're being too kind regarding Patrick Roarke. He was a vicious, small-minded bully and a petty criminal with delusions of grandeur. I hated him with every breath I took. So you see, I resent, quite strongly resent, being expected to pay for his many sins. I've plenty of my own, so if you want to try to put my head on a platter, just pick one. We'll work from there."

"Do you think because you wear a ten-thousand-dollar suit I can't smell the gutter on you?" Color began to flood Skinner's face, but when Hayes stepped forward, Skinner gestured him back with one sharp cut of the hand. "You're the same as he was. Worse, because he didn't pretend to be anything other than the useless piece of garbage he was. Blood tells."

"It may have once."

"You've made a joke out of the law, and now you hide behind a woman and a badge she's shamed."

Slowly now, Roarke got to his feet. "You know nothing of her. She's a miracle that I can't, and wouldn't, explain to the likes of you. But I can promise you, I hide behind nothing. You stand there, with fresh blood on your hands, behind your shield of blind righteousness and your memories of old glory. Your mistake, Skinner, was in trusting a man like my father to hold a bargain. And mine, it seems, was thinking you'd deal with me. So here's a warning for you."

He broke off as Hayes shifted. Fast as a rattler, Roarke drew a hand laser out of his pocket. "Take your bloody hand out of your coat while you still have one."

"You've no right, no authority to carry and draw a weapon."

Roarke stared at Skinner's furious face, then grinned. "What weapon? On your belly, Hayes, hands behind your head. Do it!" he ordered when Hayes shot Skinner a look. "Even on low these things give a nasty little jolt." He lowered the sight to crotch level. "Especially when they hit certain sensitive areas of the anatomy."

Though his breathing was now labored, Skinner gestured toward Hayes.

"To the warning. You step back from my wife. Step well and cleanly back, or you'll find the taste of me isn't to your liking."

"Will you have me beat to death in a stairwell?"

"You're a tedious man, Skinner," Roarke said with a sigh as he backed to the door. "Flaming tedious. I'd tell your men to have a care how they strut around and finger their weapons. This is my place."

Despite its size, Eve found the living area of the suite as stifling as a closed box. If she were on a case like this in New York, she would be on the streets, cursing at traffic as she fought her way to the lab to harass the techs, letting her mind shuffle possibilities as she warred with Rapid Cabs on the way to the morgue or back into Central.

The sweepers would tremble when she called demanding a final report. And the asses she would kick on her way through the investigation would be familiar.

This time around Darcia Angelo got to have all the fun.

"Peabody, go down and record Skinner's keynote, since he's playing the show must go on and giving it on schedule."

"Yes, sir."

The morose tone had Eve asking, "What?"

"I know why you're leaning toward him for this, Dallas. I can see the angles, but I just can't adjust the pattern for them. He's a legend. Some cops go wrong because the pressure breaks them inside, or because of the temptations or just because they were bent that way to begin with. He never went wrong. It's an awful big leap to see him tossing aside everything he's stood for and killing one of his own to frame Roarke for something that happened when Roarke was a kid."

"Come up with a different theory, I'll listen. If you can't do the job, Peabody, tell me now. You're on your own time here."

"I can do the job." Her voice was as stiff as her shoulders as she started for the door. "I haven't been on my own time since I met you."

Eve set her teeth as the door slammed, and was already formulating the dressing-down as she marched across the room. Mira stopped her with a word.

"Eve. Let her go. You have to appreciate her position. It's difficult being caught between two of her heroes."

"Oh, for Christ's sake."

"Sit, before you wear a rut in this lovely floor. You're in a difficult position as well. The man you love, the job that defines you, and another man who you believe has crossed an indelible line."

"I need you to tell me if he could have crossed that line. I know what my gut tells me, what the pattern of evidence indicates. It's not enough. I have data on him. Most of it's public domain, but not all." She waited a beat while Mira simply continued to study her, calm as a lake. "I'm not going to tell you how I accessed it."

"I'm not going to ask you. I already know quite a bit about Douglas Skinner. He is a man devoted to justice—his own vision of it, one who has dedicated his life to what the badge stands for, one who has risked his life to serve and protect. Very much like you."

"That doesn't feel like much of a compliment right now."

"There is a parting of the ways between you, a very elemental one. He's compelled, has always been compelled, to spread his vision of justice like some are compelled to spread their vision of faith. You, Eve, at your core, stand for the victim. He stands for his vision. Over time, that vision has narrowed. Some can become victims of their own image until they become the image."

"He's lost the cop inside the hype."

"Cleanly said. Peabody's view of him is held by a great many people, a great many in law enforcement. It's not such a leap, psychologically speaking, for me to see him as becoming so obsessed by a mistake—and the mistake was his own—that cost the lives of men in his command that that failure becomes the hungry monkey on his back."

"The man who's dead wasn't street scum. He was a young employee, one with a clean record, with a wife. The son of one of Skinner's dead. That's the leap I'm having trouble with, Dr. Mira. Was the monkey so hungry that Skinner could order the death of an innocent man just to feed it?"

"If he could justify it in his mind, yes. Ends and means. How worried are you about Roarke?"

"He doesn't want me to worry about him," Eve answered.

"I imagine he's much more comfortable when he can worry about you. His father was abusive to him."

"Yeah. He's told me pieces of it. The old man knocked hell out of him, drunk or sober." Eve dragged a hand through her hair, walked back toward the window. There was barely a hint of sky traffic.

How, she wondered, did people stand the quiet, the stillness?

"He had Roarke running cons, picking pockets, then he'd slap him around if he didn't bring home enough. I take it his father wasn't much good at the rackets because they lived in a slum."

"His mother?"

"I don't know. He says he doesn't know either. It doesn't seem to matter to him." She turned back, sat down across from Mira. "Can that be? Can it really not matter to him what his father did to him, or that his mother left him to that?"

"He knows his father started him on the path of, let's say circumventing the law. That he has a predisposition for violence. He learned how to channel it, as you did. He had a goal—to get out, to have means and power. He accomplished that. Then he found you. He understands where he came from, and I imagine it's part of his pride that he became the kind of man a woman like you would love. And, knowing his . . . profile," Mira said with a smile. "I imagine he's determined to protect you and your career in this matter, every bit as much as you're determined to protect him and his reputation."

"I don't see how . . ." Realization hit, and Eve was just getting to her feet when Roarke walked in the door.

"Goddamn it. Goddamn it, Roarke. You went after Skinner."

6

"*Good morning, Dr. Mira.*" *Roarke closed the door behind* him, then walked over to take Mira's hand. The move was as smooth as his voice, and his voice smooth as cream. "Can I get you some more tea?"

"No." Her lips twitched as she struggled to control a chuckle. "Thanks, but I really have to be going. I'm leading a seminar right after the keynote session."

"Don't think you can use her as a shield. I told you to stay away from Skinner."

"That's the second time someone's accused me of hiding behind a woman today." Though his voice remained mild, Eve knew the edge was there. "It's getting annoying."

"You want annoying?" Eve began.

"You'll have to forgive her," Roarke said to Mira as he walked her to the door. "Eve tends to become overexcited when I disobey."

"She's worried about you," Mira said under her breath.

"Well, she'll have to get over it. Have a good session." He nudged Mira out the door, closed it. Locked it. Turned. The edge was visible now. "I don't need a fucking shield."

"That was a figure of speech, and don't change the subject. You went at Skinner after I told you to stay clear of him."

"I don't take orders from you, Eve. I'm not a lapdog."

"You're a civilian," she shot back.

"And you're a consultant on someone else's case, and your authority here, in my bloody world, is a courtesy."

She opened her mouth, closed it. Hissed. Then she turned on her heel, strode out through the terrace doors, and kicked the railing several times.

"Feel better now?"

"Yes. Because I imagined it was your stupid, rock-hard head." She didn't look back, but braced her hands on the railing and looked out over what was indeed one of Roarke's worlds.

It was lavish and extravagant. The slick spears of other hotels, the tempting spreads of casinos, theaters, the glitter of restaurants were all perfectly placed. There were fountains, the silver ribbons of people glides, and the lush spread of parks where trees and flowers grew in sumptuous profusion.

She heard the click of his lighter, caught the scent of his obscenely expensive tobacco. He rarely smoked these days, she thought.

"If you'd told me it was important for you to have a face-to-face with Skinner, I'd have gone with you."

"I'm aware of that."

"Oh, Christ. Men. Look, you don't need to hide behind me or anybody. You're a tough, badass son of a bitch with a really big penis and balls of titanium steel. Okay?"

He cocked his head. "One minute. I'm imagining throwing you off the balcony. Yes." He nodded, took a long drag on the cigarette. "That's indeed better."

"If Skinner took a couple of pops at your ego, it's because he knew it was a good target. That's what cops do. Why don't you just tell me what happened?"

"He made it clear, while Hayes stood there with a hand inside his coat and on his weapon, that my father was garbage and by association so am I. And that it was long past time for my comeuppance, so to speak."

"Did he say anything that led to him ordering Weeks killed?"

"On the contrary, he twice pointed the finger at me. Full of barely restrained fury and seething emotion. You could almost believe he meant it. I don't think he's well," Roarke continued and crushed out his cigarette. "Temper put a very unhealthy color in his face, strained his breathing. I'll have to take a pass through his medical records."

"I want to take a pass at his wife. Angelo agreed, after some minor complaints, to set it up so we can double-team her later this afternoon. Meanwhile, Peabody's on Skinner, between us we'll track down the uniform, and Feeney's running names. Somebody on your security staff worked that bypass. We find out who, we link them back to Skinner and get them into interview, we change the complexion of this. Maybe put it away before ILE comes in."

She glanced back toward the suite as the 'link beeped. "Are we okay now?"

"We seem to be."

"Good. Maybe that's Angelo with the setup for Belle Skinner." She moved past Roarke to the 'link. Rather than Darcia's exotic face, Feeney's droopy one blipped on screen.

"Might have something for you here. Zita Vinter, hotel security. She was in Control between twenty-one-thirty and twenty-three hundred last night. Crossed her with your list. Popped to Vinter, Detective Carl, Atlanta cop under Skinner. Line of duty during the botched bust. Vinter's wife was pregnant with their second kid—a son, Marshall, born two months after his death. Older kid was five. Daughter, Zita."

"Bull's-eye. What sector is she in now?"

"She didn't come in today. Didn't call in either, according to her supervisor. Got her home address. Want me to ride with you?"

She started to agree, then looked back at Roarke. "No, I got it. See what else you can find on her, okay? Maybe you can tag Peabody when the keynote crap's over. She's good at digging background details. Owe you one, Feeney. Let me have the address."

After she'd ended transmission, Eve hooked her thumbs in her front pockets and looked at Roarke. "You wouldn't know where 22 Athena Boulevard might be, would you?"

"I might be able to find it, yes."

"I bet." She picked up her palm-link from the desk, stuck it in her pocket. "I'm not riding in a limo to go interview a suspect. It's unprofessional. Bad enough I'm taking some civilian wearing a fancy suit with me."

"Then I'll just have to come up with some alternate transportation."

"While you're at it, dig up your file on Zita Vinter, security sector."

He drew out his palm PC as they started out. "Always a pleasure to work with you, Lieutenant."

"Yeah, yeah." She stepped into the private elevator while he ordered something called a GF2000 brought to a garage slot. "Technically, I should contact Angelo and update her."

"No reason you can't. Once we're on the way."

"No reason. Saves time this way."

"That's your story, darling, and we'll stick to it. Vinter, Zita," he began as she scowled at him. "Twenty-eight. Two years with Atlanta PSD, then into private security. She worked for one of my organizations in Atlanta. Clean work record. Promoted to A Level over two years ago. She put in for the position here six months ago. She's single, lives alone. Lists her mother as next of kin. Her employment jacket's clean."

"When did you contract for this convention deal?"

"Just over six months ago," he said as they stepped off into the garage. "It was one of the incentives to have several of the facilities complete."

"How much do you want to bet Skinner's kept in close contact with his dead detective's daughter over the years? Angelo finesses a warrant for Vinter's 'link records, we're going to find transmissions to and from Atlanta. And not just to her mother."

When he stopped, put his PC away, she stared. "What the hell is this?"

Roarke ran a hand over the sleek chrome tube of the jetbike. "Alternate transportation."

It looked fast and it looked mean, a powerful silver bullet on two silver wheels. She continued to stare as Roarke offered her a crash helmet.

"Safety first."

"Get a grip on yourself. With all your toys I know damn well you've got something around here with four wheels and doors."

"This is more fun." He dropped the helmet onto her head.

"And I'm forced to remind you that part of this little interlude was meant to be a bit of a holiday for us."

He took a second helmet, put it on. Then tidily fastened hers. "This way you can be my biker bitch." When she showed her teeth, he only laughed and swung a leg nimbly over the tube. "And I mean that in the most flattering way possible."

"Why don't I pilot, and you can be my biker bitch?"

"Maybe later."

Swearing, she slid onto the bike behind him. He glanced back at her as she adjusted her seat, cupped her hands loosely at his hips. "Hang on," he told her.

He shot like a rocket out of the garage, and her arms latched like chains around his waist. "Lunatic!" she shouted as he blasted into traffic. Her heart flipped into her throat and stayed there while he swerved, threaded, streaked.

It wasn't that she minded speed. She liked to go fast, when she was manning the controls. There was a blur of color as they careened around an island of exotic wildflowers. A stream of motion when they rushed by a people glide loaded with vacationers. Grimly determined to face her death without blinking, she stared at the snag of vehicular traffic dead ahead.

Felt the boost of thrusters between her legs. "Don't you—"

She could only yip and try not to choke on her own tongue as he took the jet-bike into a sharp climb. Wind screamed by her ears as they punched through the air.

"Shortcut," he shouted back to her, and there was laughter in his voice as he brought the bike down to the road again, smooth as icing on cake.

He braked in front of a blindingly white building, shut off all engines. "Well, then, it doesn't come up to sex, but it's definitely in the top ten in the grand scheme."

He swung off, removed his helmet.

"Do you know how many traffic violations you racked up in the last four minutes?"

"Who's counting?" He pulled off her helmet, then leaned down to bite her bottom lip.

"Eighteen," she informed him, pulling out her palm 'link to contact Darcia Angelo. She scanned the building as she relayed a message to Darcia's voice mail. Clean, almost brutally clean. Well constructed, from the look of it, tasteful and likely expensive.

"What do you pay your security people?"

"A Level?" They crossed the wide sidewalk to the building's front entrance. "About twice what a New York police lieutenant brings in annually, with a full benefit package, of course."

"What a racket." She waited while they were scanned at the door and Roarke coded in his master. The requisite computer voice welcomed him and wished him a safe and healthy day.

The lobby was tidy and quiet, really an extended foyer with straight lines and no fuss. At the visitors' panel, Eve identified herself and requested Zita Vinter.

I'm sorry, Dallas, Lieutenant Eve, Ms. Vinter does not respond. Would you care to leave a message at this time?

"No, I don't care to leave a message at this time. This is police business. Clear me into Apartment Six-B."

I'm sorry, Dallas, Lieutenant Eve, your credentials are not recognized on this station and do not allow this system to bypass standard privacy and security regulations.

"How would you like me to bypass your circuits and stuff your motherboard up your—"

Warning! Verbal threats toward this system may result in arrest, prosecution, and monetary fines up to five thousand credits.

Before Eve could spit out a response, Roarke clamped a hand on her shoulder. "This is Roarke." He laid his hand on the palm plate. "ID 151, Level A. You're ordered to clear me and Lieutenant Dallas to all areas of this compound."

Identification verified. Roarke and companion, Dallas, Eve, are cleared.

"Lieutenant," Eve said between her teeth as Roarke pulled her toward an elevator.

"Don't take it personally. Level six," he ordered.

"Damn machine treated me like a civilian." The insult of it was almost beyond her comprehension. "A *civilian*."

"Irritating, isn't it?" He strolled off onto the sixth floor.

"You enjoyed that, didn't you? That 'Roarke and companion' shit."

"I did, yes. Immensely." He gestured. "Six–B." When she said nothing, he rang the buzzer himself.

"She didn't answer before, she's not going to answer now."

"No." He dipped his hands lightly in his pockets. "Technically . . . I suppose you need to ask Chief Angelo to request a warrant for entry."

"Technically," Eve agreed.

"I am, however, the owner of this building, and the woman's employer."

"Doesn't give you any right to enter her apartment without legal authority or permission."

He simply stood, smiled, waited.

"Do it," Eve told him.

"Welcome to my world." Roarke keyed in his master code, then hummed when the lock light above the door remained red. "Well, well, she appears to have added a few touches of her own, blocked the master code. I'm afraid that's a violation of her lease agreement."

Eve felt the little twist in her gut and slipped her hand under her jacket to her weapon. "Get in."

Neither questioned that whatever methods had been taken, he could get around them. Through them. He took a small case of tools out of his pocket and removed the anti-intruder panel on the scanner and identification plate.

"Clever girl. She's added a number of tricky little paths here. This will take a minute."

Eve took out her 'link and called Peabody. "Track down Angelo," she ordered. "We're at 22 Athena Boulevard. Six-B. She needs to get over here. I want you with her."

"Yes, sir. What should I tell her?"

"To get here." She dropped the 'link back in her pocket, stepped back to Roarke just as the lock lights went green. "Move aside," she ordered and drew her weapon.

"I've been through a door with you before, Lieutenant." He took the hand laser out of his pocket, and ignored her snarl when she spotted it. "You prefer low, as I recall."

Since there wasn't any point in biting her tongue or slapping at him for carrying, she did neither. "On my count." She put a hand on the door, prepared to shove it open.

"Wait!" He caught the faint hum, and the sound sent his

heart racing. The panel lights flashed red as he yanked Eve away from the door. They went down in a heap, his body covering hers.

She had that one breathless second to understand before the explosion blasted the door outward. A line of flame shot into the air, roaring across the hall where they'd been standing seconds before. Alarms screamed, and she felt the floor beneath her tremble at a second explosion, felt the blast of vicious heat all over her.

"Jesus! Jesus!" She struggled under him, slapped violently at the smoldering shoulder of his jacket with her bare hands. "You're on fire here."

Water spewed out of the ceiling as he sat up, stripped off the jacket. "Are you hurt?"

"No." She shook her head, shoved the hair soaked with the flood of the safety sprinklers out of her face. "Ears are ringing some. Where are you burned?" Her hands were racing over him as she pushed up to her knees.

"I'm not. The suit's fucked is all. Here, now. We're fine." He glanced back at the scarred and smoldering hole that had been the doorway. "But I'm afraid I'm going to have to evict Six-B."

Though she doubted it was necessary, Eve kept her weapon out as she picked her way over still smoking chunks of wall and door. Smoke and wet clogged the air in the hall, in the apartment, but she could see at one glance that the explosion had been smaller than she'd assumed. And very contained.

"A little paint and you're back in business."

"The explosion was set to blow the door, and whoever was outside it." There were bits of broken crockery on the floor, and a vase of flowers had fallen over, spilling water into the rivers already formed by the sprinkler system.

The furniture was sodden, the walls smeared with streaks from smoke and soot. The hallway walls were a dead loss, but otherwise, the room was relatively undamaged.

Ignoring the shouts and voices from outside the apartment, he moved through it with Eve.

Zita was in bed, her arms crossed serenely across her chest. Holstering her weapon, Eve walked to the bed, used two fingers to check for the pulse in the woman's throat.

"She's dead."

7

"*Your definition of cooperation and teamwork apparently differs from mine, Lieutenant.*"

Wet, filthy, and riding on a vicious headache, Eve strained while Darcia completed her examination of the body. "I updated you."

"No, you left a terse message on my voice mail." Darcia straightened. With her sealed hands, she lifted the bottle of pills on the nightstand, bagged them. "When you were, apparently, at the point of illegally entering this unit."

"Property owner or his representative has the right to enter a private home if there is reasonable cause to believe a life or lives may be in danger, or that said property is threatened."

"Don't quote your regulations at me," Darcia snapped. "You cut me out."

Eve opened her mouth, then blew out a long breath. "Okay, I wouldn't say I cut you out, but I did an end run around you. In your place, I'd be just as pissed off. I'm used to being able to pursue a line on an investigation in my own way, on my own time."

"You are not primary on this case. I want this body bagged and removed," Darcia ordered the uniforms flanking the bedroom doors. "Probable cause of death, voluntary self-termination."

"Wait a minute, wait a minute. Wait!" Eve ordered, throwing out a hand to warn the uniforms back. "This isn't self-termination."

"I see an unmarked body, reclining in bed. Hair neatly brushed, cosmetic enhancements unblemished. I see on the bedside table a glass of white wine and a bottle of pills prescribed for use in painless, gentle self-termination. I have here," she continued, holding up another evidence bag containing a single sheet of paper, "a note clearly stating the subject's intention to end her own life due to her guilt about her part in the death of Reginald Weeks. A death she states was ordered by Roarke and for which she was paid fifty thousand, in cash. I see a satchel containing that precise amount of cash on the dresser."

"Roarke didn't order anyone's murder."

"Perhaps not. But I am accustomed to pursuing a line on an investigation in my own way. On my own time." She tossed Eve's words back at her. "Commander Skinner has lodged a complaint claiming that Roarke threatened him this morning, with words and a weapon. Security disks at the hotel verify that Roarke entered the commander's suite and remained there for seven minutes, forty-three seconds. This incident is corroborated by one Bryson Hayes, Skinner's personal assistant, who was present at the time."

There was no point in kicking something again and pretending it was Roarke's head. "Skinner's in this up to his armpits, and if you let him deflect your focus onto Roarke, you're not as smart as I thought. First things first. You're standing over a homicide, Chief Angelo. The second one Skinner's responsible for."

Darcia ordered her men away by pointing her finger. "Explain to me how this is homicide, and why I shouldn't have you taken to the first transport and removed from this station. Why I should not, on the evidence at hand, take Roarke in for interview as a suspect in the murder of Reginald Weeks." Temper pumped into her voice now, hot and sharp. "And let me make this clear: Your husband's money pays my salary. It doesn't buy me."

Eve kept her focus on Darcia. "Peabody!" As she waited for her aide to come to the room, Eve struggled with her own temper.

"Sir?"

"What do you see?"

"Ah. Sir. Female, late twenties, medium build. No sign of struggle or distress." She broke off as Eve took an evidence bag from Darcia, passed it over. "Standard barb, commonly used in self-termination. Prescription calls for four units. All are missing. Date on the bottle is two weeks ago, prescribed and filled in Atlanta, Georgia."

Eve nodded when she saw the flicker in Darcia's eyes, then handed Peabody the note.

"Apparently suicide note, with signature. Computer-generated. The statement therein is contradictory to other evidence."

"Very good, Peabody. Tell Chief Angelo how it contradicts."

"Well, Lieutenant, most people don't have self-termination drugs tucked in their med cabinets. Unless you're suffering from an incurable and painful illness, it takes several tests and legalities to access the drug."

Darcia held up a hand. "All the more reason to have them around."

"No, sir."

"Ma'am," Darcia corrected with a smirk at Eve. "In my country a female superior is addressed as 'ma'am.'"

"Yes, ma'am. It may be different in your country as to the process of accessing this sort of drug. In the States, you have to register. If you haven't—that is, if you're still alive within thirty days of filling the prescription, you're on auto-recall. The drugs are confiscated and you're required to submit to psychiatric testing and evaluation. But besides that, it doesn't play."

"Keep going, Peabody," Eve told her.

"The note claims she decided to off herself because she was guilty over events that took place last night. But she already had the drug in her possession. Why? And how? You established time of death at oh-four-hundred this morning, so she got her payoff and the guilts awful close, then the means to self-terminate just happen to be in her possession. It's way too pat, if you follow me."

She paused, and when Darcia nodded a go-ahead, pulled in a breath and kept going. "Added to that, it doesn't follow that she would rig her apartment door to an explosive, or set another in the surveillance area to destroy the security disks of the building. Added to that," Peabody continued, obviously enjoying herself now, "Roarke's profile is directly opposed to hiring out hits, especially since Dallas popped the guy, which is one of the things he admires about her. So when you add that all up, it makes that note bogus, and this unattended death becomes a probable homicide."

"Peabody." Eve dabbed an imaginary tear from her eye. "You do me proud."

Darcia looked from one to the other. Her temper was still on the raw side, which she could admit colored her logic. Or had. "Perhaps, Officer Peabody, you could now explain how person or persons unknown gained access to this unit and persuaded this trained security expert to take termination drugs without her struggling."

"Well . . ."

"I'll take over now." Eve patted her shoulder. "You don't want to blow your streak. Person or persons unknown were admitted to the unit by the victim. Most likely to pay her off or to give her the next stage of instructions. The termination drugs were probably mixed into the wine. Person or persons unknown waited for her to slip into the first stage of the coma, at which time she was carried in here, laid out nice and pretty. The note was generated, the stage set. When it was determined that victim was dead, the explosives were rigged, and person or persons unknown went on their merry way."

"She sort of sees it," Peabody added helpfully. "Not like a psychic or anything. She just walks it through with the killer. Really mag."

"Okay, Peabody. She was a tool," Eve continued. "No more, no less. The same as Weeks was a tool. She probably joined the force to honor her father, and he used that, just as he's using Roarke's father to get to him. They don't mean anything to him as people, as flesh and blood. They're just steps and stages in his twenty-three-year war."

"Maybe not tools, then," Darcia countered, "but soldiers. To some generals they are just as dispensable. Excuse us, Officer Peabody, if you please."

"Yes, ma'am. Sir."

"I want an apology." She saw Eve wince, and smiled. "Yes, I know it'll hurt, so I want one. Not for pursuing a line of investigation, and so on. For not trusting me."

"I've known you less than twenty-four hours," Eve began, then winced again. "All right, shit. I apologize for not trusting you. And I'll go one better. For not respecting your authority."

"Accepted. I'm going to have the body taken to the ME, as a probable homicide. Your aide is very well trained."

"She's good," Eve agreed, since Peabody wasn't around to hear and get bigheaded about it. "And getting better."

"I missed the date, the significance, and I shouldn't have. I believe I would have seen these things once my annoyance with you had ebbed a bit, but that's beside the point. Now, I need to question Roarke regarding his conversation with the commander this morning, and regarding his association with Zita Vinter. To keep my official records clean, you are not included in this interview. I would appreciate it, however, if you'd remain and lead my team through the examination of the crime scene."

"No problem."

"I'll keep this as brief as I can, as I imagine both you and Roarke would like to go back and get out of those damp, dirty clothes." She tugged the sleeve of Eve's jacket as she passed. "That used to be very attractive."

"*She was easier on me than I'd've been on her,*" Eve admitted as she rolled the stiffness out of her shoulders. She'd hit the floor under Roarke harder than she'd realized and figured she should take a look at the bruises.

After a long, hot shower.

Since Roarke's response to her statement was little more than a grunt as they rode up to their suite, she took his measure. He could use some cleaning up himself, she thought. He'd ditched the ruined jacket, and the shirt beneath it had taken a beating.

She wondered if her face was as dirty as his.

"As soon as we clean up," she began as she stepped out of the elevator and into the parlor. And that was as far as she got before she was pressed up against the elevator doors with his mouth ravaging hers.

Half her brain seemed to slide out through her ears. "Whoa. What?"

"Another few seconds." With his hands gripping her shoulders and his eyes hot, he looked down at her. "We wouldn't be here."

"We are here."

"That's right." He jerked the jacket halfway down her arms, savaged her neck. "That's damn right. Now let's prove it." He stripped the jacket away, ripped her shirt at the shoulder. "I want my hands on you. Yours on me."

They already were. She tugged and tore at his ruined shirt, and because her hands were busy, used her teeth on him.

Less than a foot inside the room, they dragged each other to the floor. She rolled with him, fighting with the rest of his clothes, then arching like a bridge when his mouth clamped over her breast.

Need, deep and primal, gushed through her until she moaned his name. It was always his name. She wanted more. More to give, more to take. Her fingers dug into him—hard muscle, damp flesh. The scent of smoke and death smothered under the scent of him so that it filled her with the fevered mix of love and lust that he brought to her.

He couldn't get enough. It seemed he never could, or would. All of the hungers, the appetites and desires he'd known paled to nothing against the need he had for her—for everything she was. The strength of her, physical and that uniquely tensile morality, enraptured him. Challenged him.

To feel that strength tremble under him, open for him, merge with him, was the wonder of his life.

Her breathing was short, shallow, and he heard it catch, release on a strangled gasp when he drove her over the first peak. His own blood raged as he crushed his mouth to hers again, and plunged inside her.

All heat and speed and desperation. The sound of flesh slapping, sliding against flesh mixed with the sound of ragged breathing.

She heard him murmuring something—the language of his youth, so rarely used, slid exotically around her name. The pressure of pleasure built outrageously inside her, a glorious burn in the blood as he drove her past reason with deep, hard thrusts.

She clung, clung to the edge of it. Then his eyes were locked on hers, wild and blue. Love all but swamped her.

"Come with me." His voice was thick with Ireland. "Come with me now."

She held on, and on, watching those glorious eyes go blind. Held on, and on while his body plunged in hers. Then she let go, and went with him.

Sex, Eve had discovered, could, when it was done right, benefit body, mind, and spirit. She hardly bitched at all about having to dress up to meet with Belle Skinner at a ladies' tea. Her body felt loose and limber, and while the dress Roarke handed her didn't fit her image of cop, the weapon she snugged on under the long, fluid jacket made up for it.

"Are you intending to blast some of the other women over the watercress sandwiches and petit fours?" he asked.

"You never know." She looked at the gold earrings he held out, shrugged, then put them on. "While I'm swilling tea and browbeating Belle Skinner, you can follow up on a hunch for me. Do some digging, see if Hayes was connected to any of the downed cops under Skinner's command during the botched bust. Something there too close for employer/employee relations."

"All right. Shoes."

She stared at the needle-thin heels and flimsy straps. "Is that what you call them? How come guys don't have to wear death traps like those?"

"I ask myself that same question every day." He took a long scan after she'd put them on. "Lieutenant, you look amazing."

"Feel like an idiot. How am I supposed to intimidate anyone dressed in this gear?"

"I'm sure you'll manage."

"Ladies' tea," she grumbled on the way out. "I don't know why Angelo can't just haul the woman in to her cop shop and deal."

"Don't forget your rubber hose and mini-stunner."

She smirked over her shoulder as she stepped onto the elevator. "Bite me."

"Already did."

The tea was already under way when Eve walked in. Women in flowy dresses, and some—Jesus—in hats, milled about and gathered under arbors of pink roses or spilled out onto a terrace where a harpist plucked strings and sang in a quavery voice that instantly irritated Eve's nerves.

Tiny crustless sandwiches and pink frosted cakes were arranged on clear glass platters. Shining silver pots steamed with tea that smelled, to Eve, entirely too much like the roses.

At such times she wondered how women weren't mortified to be women.

She tracked down Peabody first and was more than slightly amazed to see her stalwart aide decked out in a swirly flowered dress and a broad-brimmed straw hat with trailing ribbons.

"Jeez, Peabody, you look like a—what is it—milkmaid or something."

"Thanks, Dallas. Great shoes."

"Shut up. Run down Mira. I want her take on Skinner's wife. The two of you hang close while Angelo and I talk to her."

"Mrs. Skinner's out on the terrace. Angelo just walked in. Wow, she's got some great DNA."

Eve glanced back, nodded to Angelo. The chief had chosen to wear cool white, but rather than flowing, the dress clung to every curve.

"On the terrace," Eve told her. "How do you want to play it?"

"Subtly, Lieutenant. Subtle's my style."

Eve lifted her brows. "I don't think so."

"Interview style," Darcia said and breezed onto the terrace. She stopped, poured tea, then strolled to the table where Belle was holding court. "Lovely party, Mrs. Skinner. I know we all want to thank you for hosting this event. Such a nice break from the seminars and panels."

"It's important to remember that we're women, not just wives, mothers, career professionals."

"Absolutely. I wonder if Lieutenant Dallas and I might have a private word with you? We won't take up much of your time."

She laid a hand on the shoulder of one of the women seated at the table. Subtle, Eve thought. And effective, as the woman rose to give Darcia her chair.

"I must tell you how much I enjoyed the commander's keynote this morning," Darcia began. "So inspiring. It must be very difficult for him, and you, to deal with the convention after your tragic loss."

"Douglas and I both believe strongly in fulfilling our duties and responsibilities, whatever our personal troubles. Poor Reggie." She pressed her lips together. "It's horrible. Even being a cop's wife for half a century . . . you never get used to the shock of violent death."

"How well did you know Weeks?" Eve asked.

"Loss and shock and sorrow aren't connected only to personal knowledge, Lieutenant." Belle's voice went cool. "But I knew him quite well, actually. Douglas and I believe in forming strong and caring relationships with our employees."

Likes Angelo, Eve thought. Hates me. Okay, then. "I guess being full of shock and sorrow is the reason you eavesdropped from your bedroom instead of coming out when we notified Commander Skinner that one of his security team had been murdered."

Belle's face went very blank and still. "I don't know what you're intimating."

"I'm not intimating, I'm saying it straight out. You were in the spare room—not the master with the commander. I know you were awake, because your light was on. You heard us relay the information, but despite this close, personal relationship, you didn't come out to express your shock and loss. Why is that, Mrs. Skinner?"

"Dallas, I'm sure Mrs. Skinner has her reasons." Darcia put a light sting of censure in her voice, then turned a sympathetic smile to Belle. "I'm sorry, Mrs. Skinner. The lieutenant is, quite naturally, on edge just now."

"There's no need for you to apologize, Chief Angelo. I understand, and sympathize—to an extent—Lieutenant Dallas's desire to defend and protect her husband."

"Is that what you're doing?" Eve tossed back. "How far

would you go? How many close, personal relationships are you willing to sacrifice? Or didn't you have one with Zita Vinter?"

"Zita?" Belle's shoulders jerked, as if from a blow. "What does Zita have to do with any of this?"

"You knew her?"

"She's our godchild, of course I . . . Knew?" Every ounce of color drained out of the lovely face so that the expertly applied enhancements stood out like paint on a doll. "What's happened?"

"She's dead," Eve said flatly. "Murdered early this morning, a few hours after Weeks."

"Dead? *Dead?*" Belle got shakily to her feet, upending her teacup as she floundered for balance. "I can't—I can't talk to you now."

"Want to go after her?" Darcia asked when Belle rushed from the terrace.

"No. Let's give her time to stew. She's scared now. Over what she knows and what she doesn't know." She looked back at Darcia. "We had a pretty good rhythm going there."

"I thought so. But I imagine playing the insensitive, argumentative cop comes naturally to you."

"Just like breathing. Let's blow this tea party and go get a drink." Eve signaled to Peabody and Mira. "Just us girls."

8

In the bar, in a wide, plush booth, Eve brooded over a fizzy water. She'd have preferred the good, hard kick of a Zombie, but she wanted a clear head more than the jolt.

"You've got a smooth, sympathetic style," she said to Darcia. "I think she'll talk to you if you stay in that channel."

"So do I."

"Dr. Mira here, she's got the same deal. You'd be able to double-team her." Eve glanced toward Mira, who was sipping white wine.

"She was shocked and shaken," Mira began. "First, she'll verify the information about the death of her godchild. When she does, grief will tangle with the shock."

"So, she'll be even more vulnerable to the right questions presented in the right style."

"You're a cold one, Dallas," Darcia said. "I like that about you. I'd be very agreeable to interviewing Belle Skinner with Dr. Mira, if that suits the doctor."

"I'm happy to help. I imagine you intend to talk to Skinner again, Eve."

"With the chief's permission."

"Don't start being polite now," Darcia told her. "You'll ruin your image. He won't want to talk to you," she went on. "Whatever his feelings toward you were before, my impression is—after his keynote—he's wrapped you and Roarke together. He hates you both."

"He brought us up at his keynote?"

"Not by name, but by intimation. His inspiring, rather cheerleader-type speech took a turn at the midway point. He went into a tangent on cops who go bad, who forget their primary duties in favor of personal comforts and gains. Gestures, body language . . ." Darcia shrugged. "It was clear he was talking about this place—luxury palaces built on blood and greed, I believe he said—and you. Bedfellows of the wicked. He got very worked up about it, almost evangelical. While there were some who appeared enthusiastic and supportive of that particular line of thought, it seemed to me the bulk of the attendees were uncomfortable—embarrassed or angry."

"He wants to use his keynote to take slaps at me and Roarke, it doesn't worry me." But Eve noticed Peabody staring down into her glass. "Peabody?"

"I think he's sick." She spoke quietly, finally lifted her gaze. "Physically, mentally. I don't think he's real stable. It was hard to watch it happen this morning. He started out sort of, well, eloquent, then it just deteriorated into this rant. I've admired him all my life. It was hard to watch," she repeated. "A lot of the cops who were there stiffened up. You could almost feel layers of respect peeling away. He talked about the murder some, how a young, promising man had become a victim of petty and soulless revenge. How a killer could hide behind a badge instead of being brought to justice by one."

"Pretty pointed," Eve decided.

"A lot of the terrestrial cops walked out then."

"So he's probably a little shaky now himself. I'll take him," Eve said. "Peabody, you track down Feeney, see what other details you can dig out on the two victims and anyone else on-site who's connected with the bust in Atlanta. That fly with you, Chief Angelo?"

Darcia polished off her wine. "It does."

Eve detoured back to the suite first. She wanted a few more details before questioning Skinner again. She never doubted Roarke had already found them.

He was on the 'link when she got there, talking to his head of hotel security. Restless, Eve wandered out onto the terrace and let her mind shuffle the facts, the evidence, the lines of possibilities.

Two dead. Both victims' fathers martyred cops. And those connected to Roarke's father and to Skinner. Murdered in a world of Roarke's making, on a site filled with police officials. It was so neat, it was almost poetic.

A setup from the beginning? It wasn't a crime of impulse but something craftily, coldly planned. Weeks and Vinter had both been sacrifices, pawns placed and disgarded for the greater game. A chess game, all right, she decided. Black king against white, and her gut told her Skinner wouldn't be satisfied with a checkmate.

He wanted blood.

She turned as Roarke stepped out. "In the end, destroying you won't be enough. He's setting you up, step by step, for execution. A lot of weapons on this site. He keeps the pressure on, piles up the circumstantial so there's enough appearance that you might have ordered these hits. All he needs is one soldier willing to take the fall. I'm betting Hayes for that one. Skinner doesn't have much time to pull it off."

"No, he doesn't," Roarke agreed. "I got into his medical records. A year ago he was diagnosed with a rare disorder. It's complicated, but the best I can interpret, it sort of nibbles away at the brain."

"Treatment?"

"Yes, there are some procedures. He's had two—quietly, at a private facility in Zurich. It slowed the process, but in his case . . . He's had complications. A strain on the heart and lungs. Another attempt at correction would kill him. He was given a year. He has, perhaps, three months of that left. And of that three months, two at the outside where he'll continue to be mobile and lucid. He's made arrangements for self-termination."

"That's rough." Eve slipped her hands into her pockets. There was more—she could see it in Roarke's eyes. Something about the way he watched her now. "It plays into the rest. This one event's been stuck in his gut for decades. He wants to clear his books before he checks out. Whatever's eating at his brain has probably made him more unstable, more fanatic and less worried about the niceties. He needs to see you go down before he does. What else? What is it?"

"I went down several more layers in his case file on the bust. His follow-ups, his notes. He believed he'd tracked my father before he'd slipped out of the country again. Skinner used some connections. It was believed that my father headed west and spent a few days among some nefarious associates. In Texas. In Dallas, Eve."

Her stomach clenched, and her heart tripped for several beats. "It's a big place. It doesn't mean . . ."

"The timing's right." He walked to her, ran his hands up and down her arms as if to warm them. "Your father and mine, petty criminals searching for the big score. You were found in that Dallas alley only a few days after Skinner lost my father's trail again."

"You're saying they knew each other, your father and mine."

"I'm saying the circle's too tidy to ignore. I nearly didn't tell you," he added, resting his forehead on hers.

"Give me a minute." She stepped away from him, leaned out on the rail, stared out over the resort. But she was seeing that cold, dirty room, and herself huddled in the corner like an animal. Blood on her hands.

"He had a deal going," she said quietly. "Some deal or other, I think. He wasn't drinking as much—and it was worse for me when he wasn't good and drunk when he came back. And he had some money. Well." She took a deep breath. "Well. It plays out. Do you know what I think?"

"Tell me."

"I think sometimes fate cuts you a break. Like it says, okay, you've had enough of that crap, so it's time you fell into something nice. See what you make out of it." She turned back to him then. "We're making something out of it. Whatever they were to us, or to each other, it's what we are now that counts."

"Darling Eve. I adore you."

"Then you'll do me a favor. Keep yourself scarce for the next couple of hours. I don't want to give Skinner any opportunities. I need to talk to him, and he won't talk if you're with me."

"Agreed, with one condition. You go wired." He took a

small jeweled pin from his pocket, attached it to her lapel. "I'll monitor from here."

"It's illegal to record without all parties' knowledge and permission unless you have proper authorization."

"Is it really?" He kissed her. "That's what you get for bedding down with bad companions."

"Heard about that, did you?"

"Just as I heard that a large portion of your fellow cops walked out of the speech. Your reputation stands, Lieutenant. I imagine your seminar tomorrow will be packed."

"My . . . Shit! I forgot. I'm not thinking about it," she muttered on the way out. "Not thinking about it."

She slipped into the conference room where Skinner was leading a seminar on tactics. It was some relief to realize she'd missed the lecture and had come in during the question-and-answer period. There were a lot of long looks in her direction as she walked down the side of the room and found a seat halfway from the back.

She scoped out the setup. Skinner on stage at the podium, Hayes standing to his back and his right, at attention. Two other personal security types on his other side.

Excessive, she thought, and obviously so. The message was that the location, the situation, posed personal jeopardy for Skinner; but he was taking precautions and doing his job.

Very neat.

She raised her hand, and was ignored. Five questions passed until she simply got to her feet and addressed him. And as she rose, she noted Hayes slide a hand inside his jacket.

She knew every cop in the room caught the gesture. The room went dead quiet.

"Commander Skinner, a position of command regularly requires you to send men into situations where loss of life, civilian and departmental, is a primary risk. In such cases, do you find it more beneficial to the operation to set personal feelings for your men aside, or to use those feelings to select the team?"

"Every man who picks up a badge does so acknowledging he will give his life if need be to serve and protect. Every commander must respect that acknowledgment. Personal feelings must be weighed, in order to select the right man for the right situation. This is a matter of experience and the accumulation, through years and that experience, of recognizing the best dynamic for each given op. But personal feelings—i.e., emotional attachments, private connections, friendships, or animosities—must never color the decision."

"So, as commander, you'd have no problem sacrificing a close personal friend or connection to the success of the op?"

His color came up. And the tremor she had noticed in his hand became more pronounced. " 'Sacrificing,' Lieutenant Dallas? A poor choice of words. Cops aren't lambs being sent to slaughter. Not passive sacrifices to the greater good, but active, dedicated soldiers in the fight for justice."

"Soldiers are sacrificed in battle. Acceptable losses."

"No loss is acceptable." His bunched fist pounded the podium. "Necessary, but not acceptable. Every man who has fallen under my command weighs on me. Every child left without a father is my responsibility. Command requires this, and that the commander be strong enough to bear the burdon."

"And does command, in your opinion, require restitution for those losses?"

"It does, Lieutenant. There is no justice without payment."

"For the children of the fallen? And for the children of those who escaped the hand of justice? In your opinion."

"Blood speaks to blood." His voice began to rise, and to tremble. "If you were more concerned with justice than with your own personal choices, you wouldn't need to ask the question."

"Justice is my concern, Commander. It appears we have different definitions of the term. Do you think your goddaughter was the best choice for this operation? Does her death weigh on you now, or does it balance the other losses?"

"You're not fit to speak her name. You've whored your badge. You're a disgrace. Don't think your husband's money or threats will stop me from using all my influence to have that badge taken from you."

"I don't stand behind Roarke any more than he stands behind me." She kept talking as Hayes stepped forward and laid a hand on Skinner's shoulder. "I don't stand on yesterday's business. Two people are dead here and now. That's my priority, Commander. Justice for them is my concern."

Hayes stepped in front of Skinner. "The seminar is over. Commander Skinner thanks you for attending and regrets Lieutenant Dallas's disruption of the question-and-answer period."

People shuffled, rose. Eve saw Skinner leaving, flanked by the two guards.

"Ask me," someone commented near her, "these seminars could use more fucking disruptions."

She made her way toward the front and came up toe to toe with Hayes.

"I've got two more questions for the commander."

"I said the seminar's over. And so's your little show."

She felt the crowd milling around them, some edging close enough to hear. "You see, that's funny. I thought I came in on the show. Does he run it, Hayes, or do you?"

"Commander Skinner is a great man. Great men often need protection from whores."

A cop moved in, poked Hayes on the shoulder. "You're gonna want to watch the name-calling, man."

"Thanks." Eve acknowledged him with a nod. "I've got it."

"Don't like play cops calling a badge a whore." He stepped back, but he hovered.

"While you're protecting the great man," Eve continued, "you might want to remember that two of his front-line soldiers are in the morgue."

"Is that a threat, Lieutenant?"

"Hell, no. It's a fact, Hayes. Just like it's a fact that both of them had fathers who died under Skinner's command. What about your father?"

Furious color slashed across his cheekbones. "You know nothing of my father, and you have no right to speak of him."

"Just giving you something to think about. For some reason I get the feeling that I'm more interested in finding out who put those bodies in the morgue than you or your great man. And because I am, I will find out—before this show breaks down and moves on. That one's a promise."

9

If she couldn't get to Skinner, Eve thought, she'd get to Skinner's wife. And if Angelo and Peabody hadn't softened and soothed enough, that was too fucking bad. Damned if she was going to tiptoe around weepy women and dying men, then have to turn the case over to the interplanetary boys.

It was her case, and she meant to close it.

She knew that part of her anger and urgency stemmed from the information Roarke had given her. His father, hers, Skinner, and a team of dead cops. Skinner was right about one thing, she thought as she headed for his suite. Blood spoke to blood.

The blood of the dead had always spoken to her.

Her father and Roarke's had both met a violent end. That was all the justice she could offer to the badges lost so many years before. But there were two bodies in cold boxes. For those, whatever they'd done, she would stand.

She knocked, waited impatiently. It was Darcia who opened the door and sent Eve an apologetic little wince.

"She's a mess," Darcia whispered. "Mira's patting her hand, letting her cry over her goddaughter. It's a good foundation, but we haven't been able to build on it yet."

"Any objections to me giving the foundation a shake?"

Darcia studied her, pursed her lips. "We can try it that way, but I wouldn't shake too hard. She shatters, we're back to square one with her."

With a nod, Eve stepped in. Mira was on the sofa with Belle, and was indeed holding her hand. A teapot, cups, and countless tissues littered the table in front of them. Belle was weeping softly into a fresh one.

"Mrs. Skinner, I'm sorry for your loss." Eve sat in a chair by the sofa, leaned into the intimacy. She kept her voice quiet, sympathetic, and waited until Belle lifted swollen, red-rimmed eyes to hers.

"How can you speak of her? Your husband's responsible."

"My husband and I were nearly blown to bits by an explosive device on Zita Vinter's apartment door. A device set by her killer. Follow the dots."

"Who else had cause to kill Zita?"

"That's what we want to find out. She sabotaged the security cameras the night Weeks was murdered."

"I don't believe that." Belle balled the tissue into her fist. "Zita would never be a party to murder. She was a lovely young woman. Caring and capable."

"And devoted to your husband."

"Why shouldn't she be?" Belle's voice rose as she got to her feet. "He stepped in when her father died. Gave her his time and attention, helped with her education. He'd have done anything for her."

"And she for him?"

Belle's lips quivered, and she sat again, as if her legs quivered as well. "She would never be a party to murder. He would never ask it of her."

"Maybe she didn't know. Maybe she was just asked to deal with the cameras and nothing else. Mrs. Skinner, your husband's dying." Eve saw Belle jerk, shudder. "He doesn't have much time left, and the loss of his men is preying on him as he prepares for death. Can you sit there and tell me his behavior over the last several months has been rational?"

"I won't discuss my husband's condition with you."

"Mrs. Skinner, do you believe Roarke's responsible for something his father did? Something this man did when Roarke was a child, three thousand miles away?"

She watched tears swim into Belle's eyes again, and

leaned in. Pressed. "The man used to beat Roarke half to death for sport. Do you know what it feels like to be hit with fists, or a stick, or whatever the hell's handy—and by the person who's supposed to take care of you? By law, by simple morality. Do you know what it's like to be bloody and bruised and helpless to fight back?"

"No." The tears spilled over. "No."

"Does that child have to pay for the viciousness of the man?"

"The sins of the fathers," Belle began, then stopped. "No." Wearily, she wiped her wet cheeks. "No, Lieutenant, I don't believe that. But I know what it has cost my husband, what happened before, what was lost. I know how it's haunted him—this good, good man, this honorable man who has dedicated his life to his badge and everything it stands for."

"He can't exorcise his ghosts by destroying the son of the man who made them. You know that, too."

"He would never harm Zita, or Reggie. He loved them as if they were his own. But . . ." She turned to Mira again, gripped her hands fiercely. "He's so ill—in body, mind, spirit. I don't know how to help him. I don't know how long I can stand watching him die in stages. I'm prepared to let him go because the pain—sometimes it's so horrible. And he won't let me in. He won't share the bed with me, or his thoughts, his fears. It's as if he's divorcing me, bit by bit. I can't stop it."

"For some, death is a solitary act," Mira said gently. "Intimate and private. It's hard to love someone and stand aside while they take those steps alone."

"He agreed to apply for self-termination for me." Belle sighed. "He doesn't believe in it. He believes a man should stand up to whatever he's handed and see it through. I'm afraid he's not thinking clearly any longer. There are moments . . ."

She steadied her breathing and looked back at Eve. "There are rages, swings of mood. The medication may be partially responsible. He's never shared the job with me to any great extent. But I know that for months now, perhaps longer, Roarke has been a kind of obsession to him. As have you. You chose the devil over duty."

She closed her eyes a moment. "I'm a cop's wife, Lieutenant. I believe in that duty, and I see it all over you. He would see it, too, if he weren't so ill. I swear to you he didn't kill Reggie or Zita. But they may have been killed for him."

"Belle." Mira offered her another tissue. "You want to help your husband, to ease his pain. Tell Lieutenant Dallas and Chief Angelo what you know, what you feel. No one knows your husband's heart and mind the way you do."

"It'll shatter him. If he has to face this, it'll destroy him. Fathers and sons," she said softly, then buried her face in the tissue. "Oh, dear God."

"Hayes." It clicked for Eve like a link on a chain. "Hayes didn't lose a father during the bust. He's Commander Skinner's son."

"A single indiscretion." Tears choked Belle's voice when she lifted her head again. "During a bump in a young marriage. And so much of it my fault. My fault," she repeated, turning her pleading gaze to Mira. "I was impatient, and angry, that so much of his time, his energies went into his work. I'd married a cop, but I hadn't been willing to accept all that that meant—all it meant to a man like Douglas."

"It isn't easy to share a marriage with duty." Mira poured more tea. "Particularly when duty is what defines the partner. You were young."

"Yes." Gratitude spilled into Belle's voice as she lifted her cup. "Young and selfish, and I've done everything in my power to make up for it since. I loved him terribly, and wanted all of him. I couldn't have that, so I pushed and prodded, then I stepped away from him. All or nothing. Well. He's a proud man, and I was stubborn. We separated for six months, and during that time he turned to someone else. I can't blame him for it."

"And she got pregnant," Eve prompted.

"Yes. He never kept it from me. He never lied or tried to hide it from me. He's an honorable man." Her tone turned fierce when she looked at Eve.

"Does Hayes know?"

"Of course. Of course he knows. Douglas would never shirk his responsibilities. He provided financial support. We worked out an arrangement with the woman, and she agreed to raise the child and keep his paternity private. There was no point, no point at all in making the matter public and complicating Douglas's career, shadowing his reputation."

"So you paid for his . . . indiscretion."

"You're a hard woman, aren't you, Lieutenant? No mistakes in your life? No regrets?"

"Plenty of them. But a child—a man—might have some problem being considered a mistake. A regret."

"Douglas has been nothing but kind and generous and responsible with Bryson. He's given him everything."

Everything except his name, Eve thought. How much would that matter? "Did he give him orders to kill, Mrs. Skinner? Orders to frame Roarke for murder?"

"Absolutely not. Absolutely not. But Bryson is . . . perhaps he's overly devoted to Douglas. In the past several months, Douglas has turned to him too often, and perhaps, when Bryson was growing up, Douglas set standards that were too high, too harsh for a young boy."

"Hayes would need to prove himself to his father."

"Yes. Bryson's hard, Lieutenant. Hard and cold-blooded. You'd understand that, I think. Douglas—he's ill. And his moods, his obsession with what happened all those years ago is eating at him as viciously as his illness does. I've heard him rage, as if there's something else inside him. And during the rage he said something had to be done, some payment made, whatever the cost. That there were times the law had to make room for blood justice. Death for death. I heard him talking with Bryson, months ago, about this place. That Roarke had built it on the bones of martyred cops. That he would never rest until it, and Roarke, were destroyed. That if he died before he could avenge those who were lost, his legacy to his son was that duty."

"Pick him up." Eve swung to Darcia. "Have your people pick Hayes up."

"Already on it," Darcia answered as she switched on her communicator.

"He doesn't know." Belle got slowly to her feet. "Or he's not allowing himself to know. Douglas is convinced that Roarke's responsible for what's happened here. Convinced himself that you're part of it, Lieutenant. His mind isn't what it was. He's dying by inches. This will finish him. Have pity."

She thought of the dead, and thought of the dying. "Ask

yourself what he would have done, Mrs. Skinner, if he were standing in my place now. Dr. Mira will stay with you."

She headed out with Darcia, waited until they were well down the hall. "There should be a way to separate him from Skinner before we bag him. Take him quietly."

Darcia called for the elevator. "You're some ruthless hard-ass, aren't you, Dallas?"

"If Skinner didn't give him a direct order, there's no point in smearing him with Hayes, or making the arrest while he's around. Christ, he's a dead man already," she snapped when Darcia said nothing. "What's the fucking point of dragging him into it and destroying half a century of service?"

"None."

"I can request another interview with Skinner, draw him away far enough for you to make the collar."

"You're giving up the collar?" Darcia asked in a shocked voice as they stepped onto the elevator.

"It was never mine."

"The hell it wasn't. But I'll take it," Darcia added cheerfully. "How'd you click to the relationship between Skinner and Hayes?"

"Fathers. The case is lousy with them. You got one?"

"A father? Doesn't everyone?"

"Depends on your point of view." She stepped off the car on the main lobby level. "I'm going to round up Peabody, give you a chance to coordinate your team." She checked her wrist unit. "Fifteen minutes ought to . . . Well, well. Look who's holding court in the lobby lounge."

Darcia tracked, studied the group crowded at two tables. "Skinner looks to have recovered his composure."

"The man likes an audience. It probably pumps him up more than his meds. We could play it this way. We go over, and I apologize for disrupting the seminar. Distract Skinner, get him talking. You tell Hayes you'd like to have a word with him about Weeks. Don't want to disturb Skinner with routine questions and blah, blah. Can you take him on your own?"

Darcia gave her a bland stare. "Could you?"

"Okay, then. Let's do it. Quick and quiet."

They were halfway across the lobby when Hayes spotted them. Two beats later, he was running.

"Goddamn it, goddamn it. He's got cop instincts. Circle that way," Eve ordered, then charged the crowd. She vaulted the smooth gold rail that separated the lounge from the lobby. People shouted, spilled back. Glassware crashed as a table overturned. She caught a glimpse of Hayes as he swung through a door behind the bar.

She leaped the bar, ignoring the curses of the servers and patrons. Bottles smashed, and there was a sudden, heady scent of top-grade liquor. Her weapon was in her hand when she hit the door with her shoulder.

The bar kitchen was full of noise. A cook droid was sprawled on the floor in the narrow aisle, its head jerking from the damage done by the fall. She stumbled over it, and the blast from Hayes's laser sang over her head.

Rather than right herself, she rolled and came up behind a stainless-steel cabinet.

"Give it up, Hayes. Where are you going to go? There are innocent people in here. Drop your weapon."

"Nobody's innocent." He fired again, and the line of heat scored across the floor and finished off the droid.

"This isn't what your father wants. He doesn't want more dead piling up at his feet."

"There's no price too high for duty." A shelf of dinnerware exploded beside her, showering her with shards.

"Screw this." She sent a line of fire over her head, rolled to the left. She came up weapon first and cursed again as she lost the target around a corner.

Someone was screaming. Someone else was crying. Keeping low, she set off in pursuit. She turned toward the sound of another blast and saw a fire erupt in a pile of linens.

"Somebody take care of that!" she shouted and turned the next corner. Saw the exit door. "Shit!"

He'd blasted the locks, effectively sealing it. In frustration she rammed it, gave it a couple of solid kicks, and didn't budge it an inch.

Holstering her weapon, she made her way back out the mess and smoke. Without much hope, she ran through the lobby, out the main doors to scan the streets. By the time she'd made it to the corner, Darcia was heading back.

"Lost him. Son of a bitch. He had a block and a half on me." Darcia jammed her own weapon home. "I'd never have caught him on foot in these damn shoes. I've got an APB out. We'll net the bastard."

"Fucker smelled the collar." Furious with herself, Eve spun in a circle. "I didn't give him enough credit. He knocked some people around in the bar kitchen. Offed a droid, started a fire. He's fast and smart and slick. And he's goddamn mean on top of it."

"We'll net him," Darcia repeated.

"Damn right we will."

10

"*Lieutenant.*"

Eve winced, turned and watched Roarke walk toward her. "Guess you heard we had a little incident."

"I believe I'll just see to some damage control." Humor cut through the anger on Darcia's face. "Excuse me."

"Are you hurt?" Roarke asked Eve.

"No. But you've got a dead droid in the bar kitchen. I didn't kill it, in case you're wondering. There was a little fire, too. But I didn't start it. The ceiling damage, that's on me. And some of the, you know, breakage and stuff."

"I see." He studied the elegant facade of the hotel. "I'm sure the guests and the staff found it all very exciting. The ones who don't sue me should enjoy telling the story to their friends and relations for quite some time. Since I'll be contacting my attorneys to alert them to a number of civil suits heading our way, perhaps you'd take a moment to fill me in on why I have a dead droid, a number of hysterical guests, screaming staff, and a little fire in the bar kitchen."

"Sure. Why don't we round up Peabody and Feeney, then I can just run through it once?"

"No, I think I'd like to know now. Let's just have a bit of a walk." He took her arm.

"I don't have time to—"

"Make it."

He led her around the hotel, through the side gardens, the patio cafe, wound through one of the pool areas and into a private elevator while he listened to her report.

"So your intentions were to spare Skinner's feelings and reputation."

"Didn't work out, but, yeah, to a point. Hayes made us first glance." The minute she was in the suite, she popped open a bottle of water, glugged. Until that moment she hadn't realized the smoke had turned her throat into a raw desert of thirst. "Should've figured it. Now he's in the wind, and that's on me, too."

"He won't get off the station."

"No, he won't get off. But he might take it in mind to do some damage while he's loose. I'll need to look at the maps and plats for the resort. We'll do a computer analysis, earmark the spots he'd be most likely to go to ground."

"I'll take care of that. I can do it faster," he said before she could object. "You need a shower. You smell of smoke."

She lifted her arm, sniffed it. "Yeah, I guess I do. Since you're being so helpful, tag Peabody and Feeney, will you? I want this manhunt coordinated."

"*Too many places for him to hide.*" An hour later, Eve scowled at the wall screens and the locations the computer had selected. "I'm wondering, too, if he had some sort of backup transpo in case this turned on him, someone he's bribed to smuggle him off-site. If he gets off this station, he could go any fucking where."

"I can work with Angelo on running that angle down," Feeney said. "And some e-maneuvering can bog down anything scheduled to leave the site for a good twenty-four hours."

"Good thinking. Keep in touch, okay?"

"Will do." He headed out, rattling a bag of almonds.

"Roarke knows the site best. He'll take me around to the specified locations. We'll split them up with Angelo's team."

"Do I coordinate from here?" Peabody asked.

"Not exactly. I need you to work with Mira. Make sure

Skinner and his wife stay put and report if Hayes contacts them. Then there's this other thing."

"Yes, sir." Peabody looked up from her memo book.

"If we don't bag him tonight, you'll have to cover for me in the morning."

"Cover for you?"

"I've got the notes and whatever in here." Eve tossed her ppc into Peabody's lap.

"Notes?" Peabody stared at the little unit in horror. "Your seminar? Oh, no, sir. Uh-uh. Dallas, I'm not giving your seminar."

"Just think of yourself as backup," Eve suggested. "Roarke?" She walked to the door and through it, leaving Peabody sputtering.

"Just how much don't you want to give that seminar tomorrow?" Roarke wondered.

"I don't have to answer that until I've been given the revised Miranda warning." Eve rolled her shoulders and would have sworn she felt weight spilling off them. "Sometimes things just work out perfect, don't they?"

"Ask Peabody that in the morning."

With a laugh, she stepped into the elevator. "Let's go hunting."

They hit every location, even overlapping into Angelo's portion. It was a long, tedious, and exacting process. Later she would think that the operation had given her a more complete view of the scope of Roarke's pet project. The hotels, casinos, theaters, restaurants, the shops and businesses. The houses and buildings, the beaches and parks. The sheer sweep of the world he'd created was more than she'd imagined.

While impressive, it made the job at hand next to impossible.

It was after three in the morning when she gave it up for the night and stumbled to bed. "We'll find him tomorrow. His face is on every screen on-site. The minute he tries to buy any supplies, we'll tag him. He has to sleep, he has to eat."

"So do you." In bed, Roarke drew her against him. "Turn it off, Lieutenant. Tomorrow's soon enough."

"He won't go far." Her voice thickened with sleep. "He needs to finish it and get his father's praises. Legacies. Bloody legacies. I spent my life running from mine."

"I know." Roarke brushed the top of her head with his lips as she fell into sleep. "So have I."

This time it was he who dreamed, as he rarely did, of the alleyways of Dublin. Of himself, a young boy, too thin, with sharp eyes, nimble fingers, and fast feet. A belly too often empty.

The smell of garbage gone over, and whiskey gone stale, and the cold of the rain that gleefully seeped into bone.

He saw himself in one of those alleyways, staring down at his father, who lay with that garbage gone over, too, and smelled of that whiskey gone stale. And smelled, too, of death—the blood and the shit that spewed out of a man at his last moments. The knife had still been in his throat, and his eyes—filmed-over blue—were open and staring back at the boy he'd made.

He remembered, quite clearly, speaking.

Well now, you bastard, someone's done for ya. And here I thought it would be me one day who had the pleasure of that.

Without a qualm, he'd crouched and searched through the pockets for any coin or items that might be pawned or traded. There'd been nothing, but then again, there never had been much. He'd considered, briefly, taking the knife. But he'd liked the idea of it where it was too much to bother.

He'd stood then, at the age of twelve, with bruises still fresh and aching from the last beating those dead hands had given him.

And he'd spat. And he'd run.

He was up before she was, as usual. Eve studied him as she grabbed her first cup of coffee. It was barely seven A.M. "You look tired."

He continued to study the stock reports on one screen and the computer analysis of potential locations on another. "Do I? I suppose I could've slept better."

When she crouched in front of him, laid a hand on his thigh, he looked at her. And sighed. She could read him well enough, he thought, his cop.

Just as he could read her, and her worry for him.

"I wonder," he began, "and I don't care to, who did me the favor of sticking that knife in him. Someone, I think, who was part of the cartel. He'd have been paid, you see, and there was nothing in his pockets. Not a fucking punt or pence on him, nor in the garbage hole we lived in. So they'd have taken it, whatever he hadn't already whored or drank or simply pissed away."

"Does it matter who?"

"Not so very much, no. But it makes me wonder." He nearly didn't say the rest, but simply having her listen soothed him. "He had my face. I forget that most times, remember that I've made myself, myself. But Christ, I have the look of him."

She slid into his lap, brushed her hands through his hair. "I don't think so." And kissed him.

"We've made each other in the end, haven't we, Darling Eve? Two lost souls into one steady unit."

"Guess we have. It's good."

He stroked his cheek against hers, and felt the fatigue wash away. "Very good."

She held on another minute, then drew back. "That's enough sloppy stuff. I've got work to do."

"When it's done, why don't we get really sloppy, you and I?"

"I can get behind that." She rose to contact Darcia and get an update on the manhunt.

"Not a sign of him anywhere," Eve told Roarke, then began to pace. "Feeney took care of transpo. Nothing's left the station. We've got him boxed in, but it's a big box with lots of angles. I need Skinner. Nobody's going to know him as well as Skinner."

"Hayes is his son," Roarke reminded her. "Do you think he'd help you?"

"Depends on how much cop is left in him. Come with me," she said. "He needs to see us both. He needs to deal with it."

* * *

He looked haggard, Eve thought. His skin was gray and pasty. How much was grief, how much illness, she didn't know. The combination of the two, she imagined, would finish him.

But, she noted, he'd put on a suit, and he wore his precinct pin in the lapel.

He brushed aside, with some impatience, his wife's attempt to block Eve.

"Stop fussing, Belle. Lieutenant." His gaze skimmed over Roarke, but he couldn't make himself address the man. "I want you to know I've contacted my attorneys on Hayes's behalf. I believe you and Chief Angelo have made a serious error in judgment."

"No, you don't, Commander. You've been a cop too long. I appreciate the difficulty of your position, but Hayes is the prime suspect in two murders, in sabotage, in a conspiracy to implicate Roarke in those murders. He injured bystanders while fleeing and caused considerable property damage. He also fired his weapon at a police officer. He's currently evading arrest."

"There's an explanation."

"Yes, I believe there is. He's picked up his father's banner, Commander, and he's carrying it where I don't think you intended it to go. You told me yesterday no losses are acceptable. Did you mean it?"

"The pursuit of justice often . . . In the course of duty, we . . ." He looked helplessly at his wife. "Belle, I never meant—Reggie, Zita. Have I killed them?"

"No, no." She went to him quickly, wrapped her arms around him. And he seemed to shrink into her. "It's not your fault. It's not your doing."

"If you want justice for them, Commander, help me. Where would he go? What would he do next?"

"I don't know. Do you think I haven't agonized over it through the night?"

"He hasn't slept," Belle told her. "He won't take his pain medication. He needs to rest."

"I confided in him," Skinner continued. "I shared my thoughts, my beliefs, my anger. I wanted him to carry on my mission. Not this way." Skinner sank into a chair. "Not this way, but I beat the path. I can't deny that. Your father killed for sport, for money, for the hell of it," he said to Roarke. "He didn't even know the names of the people he murdered. I look at you and see him. You grew out of him."

"I did." Roarke nodded. "And everything I've done since has been in spite of him. You can't hate him as much as I can, Commander. No matter how hard you try, you'll never reach my measure of it. But I can't live on that hate. And I'm damned if I'll die on it. Will you?"

"I've used it to keep me alive these past months." Skinner looked down at his hands. "It's ruined me. My son is a thorough man. He'll have a back door. Someone inside who'll help him gain access to the hotel. He'll need it to finish what he started."

"Assassinate Roarke?"

"No, Lieutenant. Payment would be dearer than that. It's you he'll aim for." He lifted a hand to a face that had gone clammy. "To take away what his target cherishes most."

When he hissed in pain, Eve stepped forward. "You need medical attention, Commander. You need to be in the hospital."

"No hospitals. No health centers. Try to take him alive, Dallas. I want him to get the help he needs."

"You have to go." Belle stepped in. "He can't take any more of this."

"I'll send Dr. Mira." Even as Eve spoke, Skinner slumped in the chair.

"He's unconscious." Roarke instinctively loosened Skinner's tie. "His breathing's very shallow."

"Don't touch him! Let me—" Belle jerked back as her eyes met Roarke's. She took a long, deep breath. "I'm sorry. Could you help me, please? Take him into his bedroom. If you'd call for Dr. Mira, Lieutenant Dallas, I'd be grateful."

*"H*is body's wearing down," Eve said once Skinner was settled in the bedroom with Mira in attendance. "Maybe it's better all around if he goes before we take Hayes."

"His body was already worn down," Roarke corrected. "But he's let go of his reason to live."

"There's nothing to do but leave him to Mira. The computer didn't think Hayes would come back to the hotel. Skinner does. I'm going with Skinner. Hayes wants me, and he knows Skinner's on borrowed time so he has to move fast." She checked her wrist unit. "Looks like I'm going to give that damn seminar after all."

"And make yourself a target?"

"With plenty of shield. We'll coordinate your security people and Angelo's and pluck him like a goose if he tries for a hit here." She started out, pulling a borrowed communicator out of her pocket.

Then drew her weapon as she saw Hayes step out of the stairway door at the end of the corridor.

"Stop!" She pounded after him when he ducked back into the stairwell. "Get to security!" Eve shouted at Roarke. "Track him!"

Roarke shoved through the door ahead of her. The weapon in his hand was illegal. "No. You track him."

Since cursing was a waste of time, she raced down the stairs with him. "Subject sighted," she called through the communicator as they streaked down the stairs. "Heading down southeast stairwell, now between floors twenty-one and twenty. Moving fast. Consider subject armed and dangerous."

She clicked the communicator off before she spoke to Roarke. "Don't kill him. Don't fire that thing unless there's no choice."

A blast hit the landing seconds before their feet. "Such as now?" Roarke commented.

But it was Eve who fired, leaning over the railing and turning the steps below into rubble. Caught in midstride, Hayes tried to swing back, bolt for the door, but his momentum skewed his balance.

He went down hard on the smoking, broken steps.

And Angelo shoved through the door, weapon gripped in both hands.

"Trying to take my collar, Dallas?"

"All yours." Eve stepped down, onto the weapon that had flown out of Hayes's hand. "Two people dead. For what?" she asked Hayes. "Was it worth it?"

His mouth and his leg were bleeding. He swiped at the

blood on his chin while his eyes burned into hers. "No. I should've been more direct. I should've just blown you to hell right away and watched the bastard you fuck bleed over you. That would've been worth everything, knowing he'd live with the kind of pain his father caused. The commander could've died at peace knowing I'd found his justice. I wanted to give him more."

"Did you give Weeks or Vinter a choice?" Eve demanded. "Did you tell them they were going to die for the cause?"

"Command isn't required to explain. They honored their fathers, as I honor mine. There's no other choice."

"You signaled Weeks to move in on me, and he didn't have a clue what it was going to cost him. You had Vinter sabotage the cameras, and when she realized why, you killed her."

"They were necessary losses. Justice requires payment. You were going to be my last gift to him. You in a cage," he said to Roarke. "You in a coffin." He smiled at Eve when he said it. "Why aren't you giving your seminar, Lieutenant? Why the hell aren't you where you're scheduled to be?"

"I had a conflict of . . ." She shot to her feet. "Oh, God. Peabody."

She charged through the door and out into the corridor. "What floor? What floor?"

"This way." Roarke grabbed her hand, pulled her toward the elevator. "Down to four," he said. "We'll head left. Second door on the right takes us behind the stage area."

"Explosives. He likes explosives." She dragged out her communicator again as she willed the elevator to hurry. "She's turned hers off. Son of a bitch! Any officer, any officer, clear Conference Room D immediately. Clear the area of all personnel. Possible explosive device. Alert Explosive Division. Clear that area now!"

She was through the door and streaking to the left.

I sent her there, was all she could think. And I smirked about it.

Oh, God, please.

There was a roaring in her ears that was either her own rush of blood, the noise of the audience, or the shouted orders to clear.

But she spotted Peabody standing behind the podium and

leaped the three steps on the side of the stage. Leaped again
the minute her feet hit the ground and, hitting her aide mid-
body, shot them both into the air and into a bruised and
tangled heap on the floor.

She sucked in her breath, then lost it again as Roarke
landed on top of her.

The explosion rang in her ears, sent the floor under her
shaking. She felt the mean heat of it spew over her like a
wave that sent the three of them rolling in one ball toward
the far edge of the stage.

Debris rained over them, some of it flaming. Dimly she
heard running feet, shouts, and the sizzling hiss of a fire.

For the second time in two days, she was drenched with
the spray of overhead sprinklers.

"Are you all right?" Roarke said in her ear.

"Yeah, yeah. Peabody." Coughing, eyes stinging with
smoke, Eve eased back, saw her aide's pale face, glassy eyes.
"You okay?"

"Think so." She blinked. " 'Cept you've got two heads,
Dallas, and one of them's Roarke's. It's the prettiest. And I
think you've really gained some weight." She smiled vaguely
and passed out.

"Got herself a nice concussion," Eve decided, then turned
her head so her nose bumped Roarke's. "You are pretty,
though. Now get the hell off me. This is seriously undigni-
fied."

"Absolutely, Lieutenant."

While the med-techs tended to Peabody, and the Explosives Division cordoned off the scene, Eve sat outside the
conference room and drank the coffee some unnamed and
beloved soul had handed her.

She was soaked to the skin, filthy, had a few cuts, a medley
of bruises. She figured her ears might stop ringing by Christ-
mas.

But all in all, she felt just fine.

"You're going to have a few repairs on this dump of
yours," she told Roarke.

"Just can't take you anywhere, can I?"

She smiled, then got to her feet as Darcia approached.
"Hayes is in custody. He's waived his right to attorney. My
opinion, he'll end up in a facility for violent offenders, men-

tal defectives. He's not going to serve time in a standard cage. He's warped. If it's any consolation, he was very disappointed to hear you aren't splattered all over what's left of that stage in there."

"Can't always get what you want."

"Hell of a way to skate out of giving a workshop, though. Have to hand it to you."

"Whatever works."

Sobering, Darcia turned. "We beat interplanetary deadline. Thanks."

"I won't say anytime."

"I'll have a full report for your files by the end of the day," she said to Roarke. "I hope your next visit is less . . . complicated," she added.

"It was an experience watching you in action, Chief Angelo. I'm confident Olympus is in good hands."

"Count on it. You know, Dallas, you look like you could use a nice resort vacation." She shot out that brilliant smile. "See you around."

"She's got a smart mouth. I've got to admire that. I'm going to check on Peabody," she began, then stopped when she saw Mira coming toward her.

"He's gone," Mira said simply. "He had time to say goodbye to his wife, and to ask me to tell you that he was wrong. Blood doesn't always tell. I witnessed the termination. He left life with courage and dignity. He asked me if you would stand in the way of his departmental service and burial."

"What did you tell him?"

"I told him that blood doesn't always tell. Character does. I'm going back to his wife now."

"Tell her I'm sorry for her loss, and that law enforcement has lost one of its great heroes today."

Mira leaned over to kiss Eve's cheek, smiling when Eve squirmed. "You have a good heart."

"And clear vision," Roarke added when Mira walked away.

"Clear vision?"

"To see through the dreck and the shadows to the core of the man."

"Nobody gets through life without fucking up. He gave fifty years to the badge. It wasn't all what it should've been,

but it was fifty years. Anyway." She shook off sentiment.
"I've got to check on Peabody."

Roarke took her hand, kissed it. "We'll go check on Peabody. Then we'll talk about that nice resort vacation."

In a pig's eye, she thought. She was going home as soon as humanly possible. The streets of New York were resort enough for her.